TROUBLE COMING

Then we heard that them goddamned Bensons was out of the pen. At first that didn't worry me too much, because I had done handled them once before, and that when there had been five of them to contend with, not just only four. Besides, I figured they'd likely had just about enough of me the first time around. Then that message come over the wire. Little Herman Simpson brought it to me in the Hooch House.

"This just come in for you, Marshal Barjack," he said, looking timid as hell and holding that piece of paper out toward me, his hand a shaking.

"Well, hell, Simp," I said, "let me have the god damn thing."

I jerked it out of the little sissy's trembling hand and read it. There wasn't no words in it that I couldn't handle all right. Here's what it said:

BARJACK
WE'LL BE ON THE STREET OF ASS TOWN
AT HIGH NOON AUG 15. YOU BE THERE TOO.
BENSONS

That was all it said.

Barjack

ROBERT J. CONLEY

LEISURE BOOKS NEW YORK CITY

This book is lovingly dedicated to the memory of Bobby Jack Smith.

A LEISURE BOOK®

February 2000

Published by

Dorchester Publishing Co., Inc.
276 Fifth Avenue
New York, NY 10001

ISBN 0-8439-4687-3

Barjack

Chapter One

August 7, 1889

Everyone in the whole town of Asininity knowed that the goddamned Bensons was coming back to town, and what's more, they knowed just why the bastards was coming. They was coming in with one and only one purpose in their ugly heads, and that was to blow my ass all the way to hell.

I had been town marshal of Asininity for something like ten years by that time, and the town had been real peaceful-like for maybe the last nine and a half of them years. When I had first rode into the place, it had been a genuine hell-hole, wild and raw. Tombstone, Abilene, Dodge City, Deadwood, hell, none of them had anything on Asininity, and that's the gospel truth, I can tell you. Hell, I seen them all in their worse times. A man on the streets of Asininity in them days had a right short life expectancy, I can tell you that. I was only about thirty years old, and at that time I was pretty goddamned ornery myself. I ain't very big, only about five foot seven, and back then I weighed about a hundred and fifty pounds was all, but I was tough as old rawhide. Maybe a real quick rundown on my background will give you some idea of just how tough a little son of a bitch I really was.

I was born in 1850, away back east in Manhattan. That's in New York, you know. My folks had came over from the old country without a dime in their pockets or a pot to piss in. I ain't real sure, but looking back over what dates I know about, I think it's highly likely that I was conceived at high sea, and given the nature of my disposition and the direction my life was to take, I wouldn't be a damned bit surprised if the act had took place during a gale.

Be that as it may, the old land of milk and honey just didn't live up to its promise. No, sir. I grew up poor and tough, scrapping for a nickel or a dime or a loaf of bread, and when I was only about twelve or thirteen years old, I had myself a minor altercation one day with an Irish kid who was about twice my size. I ain't real sure after all these years, but I believe that his name was Doyle. Now, I never have been one to go in for that bull about a fair fight, especially if my opponent is bigger than me and has clearly expressed his intention to make mush out of my head.

Doyle, if that really was his name, was just standing there looking down at me all snotty and puffed up and waiting to see if I was going to cry or run away or take a swing at him or what, and I just kicked him in the balls as hard as I could kick. Well, he didn't scream, but he did double over and grab at his crotch with both hands, and his face did take on a most horrible expression of pain and anguish and turn a real sick shade of green, kind of the color of a goose turd, and he sank down real slow on his knees and then sort of tilted forward until his forehead bounced against the sidewalk.

I didn't know how long he would stay that way if I just let it go at that, and so I commenced to kicking him some more while he was down. I'm sure I stove up his ribs and deprived him of most of his front teeth before a friend of my old man's took notice of the situation and managed to calm me down just a bit by grabbing me from behind by both of my arms and pulling me away. I struggled some,

8

'cause I was in the mood just then to do some real mayhem, but he jerked on my collar real hard, yanking me clean off my feet, and he yelled at me to desist. I finally did. Doyle was just curled up on the sidewalk in a ball. He was whimpering and dripping blood into a nice red pool just below his face. I liked the look of it. I was feeling mean as hell.

"You damn little fool," said this fellow. "Do you know who his daddy is?"

"Hell, no," said I, still feeling tough and cocky, "and what's more I don't give a damn. He was bullying on me, and I just give him what he had coming to him. That's all."

"Shut up, you little smart-ass," he said, "and listen to me. His daddy is a big shot with the Five Points Gang. You know who they are, don't you?"

Well, I sure as all hell did know who they was. Everybody around knew the Five Points Gang, and everybody was scared of them too. The Five Points Gang was a vicious bunch of Irishmen, about five hundred strong, who ran the old Fourth Ward of the Lower East Side. They was made up of professional killers, pickpockets, burglars, stickup artists and general all-around bad-ass thugs. They openly walked the streets in the broad daylight with loaded pistols stuck in their belts. Well, my eyes must have bugged out, and my heart did skip a beat or two. My victim was still curled up there on the sidewalk, and he was puking his guts out by then, but when I heard who his old man was, I felt sicker than he looked. I didn't have to think very long, neither, on my situation. I figured that if I was to hang around the old neighborhood, I would wind up real dead real soon—either that or in such a condition that I'd be wishing I was dead.

"Go see my folks for me, will you?" I said. "Tell them what happened. Tell Momma I love her, and I'll write when I get to someplace safe. I'm clearing out of here while I can still run."

He promised that he would do as I had asked him to, and as he turned away from me to walk off in the direction of my folks' home, I got to thinking what a mess of trouble that damned Doyle kid had brung into my young life, and I just kicked him once more up the side of the head for good measure. Hell, I might have killed him, for all I know. Then I headed off in the other direction just about as fast as I could make my shaking legs move me.

I run straight down to the railroad yard and stowed myself away on the first baggage car I could sneak myself into. I didn't have no idea where the train was going, and I didn't care a damn, just so long as it was taking me the hell away from those goddamned Irish bastards. Now, I should say before I go on farther with my story that I ain't got nothing against the Irish, just them Five Pointers, that's all. And them bastards did send me off on a long life of trouble. 'Course, at the same time, they might have did my folks a big favor, since I was leaving them with one less mouth to feed and one less kid to try to keep out of trouble.

Well, it was a long and a rough ride, and I begun to think that I was fated to starve to death alone in that baggage car while jiggling along headed toward some unknown destination. I even thought for a while that I'd have been better off to have stayed at home and took my chances with the Five Points Gang. But I knowed better than that. Likely the way they'd have killed me would have been just as slow as starving and likely considerable more painful, like maybe they'd have broke each bone in my whole body one at a time or something like that. Now, I ain't going to go on with all the details of that miserable railroad trip. The main thing is that I got caught, and I was all set up to be throwed in jail, and at my tender age too, but I come up with a scheme. I started in to crying and wailing.

"I'm just a poor orphan boy," I said between sobs and lying like hell, "and I didn't mean to steal me no ride. Honest I didn't. I'm broke and I'm hungry, and I was just looking for a job with the railroad, that's all, and I got sort of lost. I ain't even real sure how I wound up in that old baggage car, and I don't even know where we're at neither."

Well, by God, I couldn't hardly believe it, but they called

my bluff, and I wound up with a crew in Missouri laying tracks for the Katy—that's the M.K. and T. Railroad, in case you didn't know it. And that's how I wound up out in the woolly West. Hell, I was doing a man's work, and I was damn sure keeping up my end of it, too. I can tell you, boys, that driving them spikes will put some muscles on you. If I had thought that I was tough back there in Manhattan, well, hell, I just thought it, that's all. I didn't know what tough was until I'd spent a season laying track for the Katy.

Well, we was busy at work laying track one day out in western Missouri, when all of a sudden and without no warning a whole gang of ruffians come down on us a-shooting and a-whooping and a-hollering. The man right next to me dropped dead with a bullet smack between his eyes. Well, that scared the hell out of me for sure. I like to pissed my pants, and I turned tail and run like the very devil was after my ass with his pitchfork. I hid myself behind a big oak tree, and I hugged it for dear life, and I watched while them owlhoots massacred the whole entire crew right there in front of my eyes. Once their butchery was over and done, they commenced searching all the pockets of all the dead men and stealing everything they could get their hands on.

I was still just watching wide-eyed all the goings-on, scared to death to move a muscle, and wondering what the hell was going to become of me, just thirteen years old and left alone out in the wild Missouri woods, when all of a sudden I felt a couple of big, rough hands grab onto me from behind. I let out an awful yelp and started in to kicking and wriggling, trying to break myself loose from the big ape, but he had a powerful hard grip, and I couldn't shake him. Pretty soon, though, he had me out there in front of the whole gang, and when I seen them mean-eyeing me, and they closed in around me in a tight circle, I kind of settled down.

"You want me to cut his throat?" the one that had ahold of me said.

"Nah," said a scar-faced fellow who was standing right

11

in front of me and giving me a look. "Hell, he's just a snot-nosed kid. What're you doing out here anyway, kid?"

I thought real quick, trying to figure out what kind of story might most appeal to these savage galoots. "I'm just a poor orphan," I said. "I ain't got no home, and so I hitched me a ride on a railroad car. Then the railroad dicks caught me, and they put me to work here with this crew. I didn't have no choice in the matter. Hell, it's like slave labor."

Well, that done the trick. They all got a good laugh and said that I was awful pale to be in that situation, and so the scar-faced bastard decided that he'd give me a home—if you could call running with the gang and sleeping in camps and such a home. His name was Butcher Henshaw. Well, I don't reckon that was the name his momma give him at birth, but that was all I ever heard him called. Old Butcher and his boys called themselves Confederate guerillas and irregulars, but really they wasn't nothing but a gang of outlaws using the current civil unrest as a cover-up for their criminal activities.

But I guess, looking back on it all, there couldn't have been no better home for a lad such as I was in them days. I was alone without my family in a wild country that I didn't know a damn thing about. Old Butcher took me under his wing, so to speak, and commenced to raise me up just like I had been his own kid. He taught me to ride a horse like a Comanche. I could hang off to one side and shoot under the critter's neck while at the same time not presenting myself as a target for the other fellow. I liked that pretty good. And he taught me to shoot six-guns with both hands and to handle a rifle for long shots. I got a real good raising-up from old Butcher. Hell, I guess I owe a lot to him.

We never managed to pull off a real big job to make old Butcher world famous such as the likes of old Willie Quantrell or Jim Lane or Bloody Bill. We never done nothing as spectacular as the raid on Lawrence, Kansas, but we hit a bunch of smaller towns and robbed their banks and emptied the pockets of all their citizens—all, of course, in the name of the grand cause of the Confederate States of America. I didn't know a damn thing about what that meant, and I never heard Butcher nor none of the boys talk about it neither. I just figured that the only grand cause we was really serving was just the cause of our own pockets, and that was all. It didn't bother my conscience none, though, knowing that.

And our pockets was jingling a good many days, and whenever they was, we really did live it up high on the hog. Old Butcher introduced me at an early age to good whiskey and the pleasures of whores and such. And I guess I could have stayed perfect content with that life if it had lasted. But good things never does, it seems, and one day in '65, I think it was, I must have reached fifteen years by then, and we was on our way to make another little raid to line our pockets. We had stopped and set up camp for the night, figuring that we had about half a day's ride left ahead of us. Butcher said we'd crawl out early in the morning, have us all a good breakfast, and hit that little hamlet right about noontime.

All of a sudden it sounded like the forces of hell had came together and was riding down on us, and the boys was all scrambling for their guns and tripping over their blankets, and the horses was a-screaming and a-stamping. I grabbed the old Springfield rifle that Butcher had give me and run for the nearest tree to hide behind. The attackers was all regular Union army troops, and they wasn't showing no mercy. I seen Butcher take down four or five of them soldier boys all by hisself before one of them run a cavalry saber in between his ribs. Well, I took dead aim and blowed a hole in that son of a bitch's back 'most near big enough to ride a horse through, and I was lucky, too, that no one noticed where the shot had come from. It was mighty near getting dark, and I just lay low there till all the furor was through, and the Yankees rode off feeling all proud of their grand accomplishments.

When I felt for sure that it was safe, I come out from my hidey-hole and poked around amongst the wreckage and the carnage of the camp. I didn't find no one alive, but

I did manage to find a revolver and some ammunition for it that the blue-bellies had overlooked and left laying there. I found myself some food too, and I et it. Well, there I was again, all alone in the world, but this time I had acquired myself some surviving skills, and I had me a six-gun, a rifle gun, and some bullets, and my belly was full. I decided that I'd get myself away from that bloody spot. I didn't fancy sleeping the night amongst corpses, not even if they had been my friends, and, by God, my luck held out on me some more. I hadn't walked far from camp before I come across one of our horses that had ran off when the shooting started. He was still saddled and ready to ride, and I caught him up real easy too.

In the years in between then and when I finally rode into Asininity for the first time, I done a bunch of things. I punched cows, but I never cared for that too much. The days was too long, and it was too many days between a trip to town for drinking and whoring. The pay wasn't much, neither, so I up and quit and swore that I didn't want nothing to do with cows no more other than to eat a steak every now and then. I just couldn't see no future in cowboying. I was a hide-hunter then for a while, and I made some pretty good money there, but I was too full of buffalo-skinning stink all the time. I got to where I couldn't hardly stand to smell myself, so I knowed for sure that no one else wanted to be near enough to get a whiff of me. I give up that career and took me a hot bath in a tub with suds each day for a week. Then I drove a freight wagon for a spell, and I done me some hard-rock mining, but both of them occupations didn't consist of nothing but hard work, and that kind of activity never did set too well with me.

I was even a half-assed mountain man for a spell, not by choice, but I reckon the lowest I ever did sink was once when I was real down and out, flat busted and hungry, I actual become a low-down bounty man. I hunted down old Six-toes Craddock down in the Indian Territory and snuck up on him in the dark one night right there at his own campsite and blowed a great big hole in the bastard's back. Then I pulled off his boots, and, by God, he really did have

14

six toes on each foot, and that's the only way I was able to get his body positively identified so as I could collect the reward I rightfully had coming to me for a job well done. They give me fifty dollars for old Six-toes's stiff.

With that success under my belt and giving me a real swell head, I decided that I'd go after bigger fish and earn me some real money. Applesauce Jackson was giving the law fits around there about that time, and they had five hundred dollars on him, dead or alive. That was the way I liked them. Old Applesauce had once been a deputy U.S. marshal working for old Judge Parker out of Fort Smith, Arkansas, but he had gone bad. There was several stories about how that had came about, but the one I heard the most and put the most trust in was that he got caught selling whiskey to Cheyenne Indians. Well, they took his badge away from him and fined him some, and he took to robbing trains.

From there he become a full-fledged outlaw, and because he was a lawman turned owlhoot, I guess they wanted him particular bad. He had killed a few folks too, from what they said, all in the course of robberies, though. He hadn't never done no cold-blooded deliberate murders. He wasn't especially mean like that. He was just an outlaw, was all. But I set my sights on old Applesauce. By the way, I never did hear anything about how he got that name of Applesauce, but anyhow I set about to tracking him.

I followed up a number of false leads, and I was running low on cash, so I was just about to give it up and look for some other line of work, when I run right smack into him in a little town in Kansas just across the line from the Indian nations. He was setting at a table in the corner of a saloon a-sipping whiskey, and he had a little whore setting on his lap. I thought that would be about as fine a time to take advantage of as I was likely to have, for one hand was holding his whiskey glass and the other one was under the table, I figured busy fondling certain sweet parts of that gal's anatomy.

I pulled the dodger on Applesauce out of my pocket and looked at his picture one more time. Then I looked back at him. I had the right man, sure enough. There couldn't be no mistake in it. His ears stuck straight out from the sides of his head, and they was big ones, too. I never seen a pair like that before or since. And he wore a real droopy mustache. On top of all that, his nose was somewhat too large for the rest of his face and was shaped kind of like an eagle's beak or something like that. I folded that dodger up and put it back in my pocket. Then I walked straight for him.

I was about halfway across the floor when he seen me coming, and he didn't do nothing but only just look at me. That whore just kept giggling and kissing his cheek and nibbling on his big ear. I come up to within a couple of paces of his table, and he was looking at me from across on the other side.

"You'd be Applesauce Jackson," I said.

"So what?" he said. "Who're you?"

"Name's Barjack," I said, and I pulled out my revolver and pointed it at him. I was thinking he never had a chance, the fool, with his hands busy with whiskey and a woman setting on his lap. I should have just shot him dead right then and there, but there was a whole room full of folks a-watching, and even though he was wanted dead or alive, and I always figured that meant preferably dead, I might have got frowned on for just shooting him like that. With my left hand I pulled out the dodger again, and I tossed it on the table in front of him.

He didn't reach out to pick it up, the way I thought he might. Instead, he just kept looking straight at me, and "I seen one before," he said.

"You're a wanted man," I said, "and I aim to take you in for the reward. Now, if you'll just reach your both hands up over your head—"

"Barjack," he said. "I've got a forty-five under the table, cocked and aimed at your crotch. You sure you want to go through with this?"

It didn't take me long to think over the situation I was in. "No," I told him, "I ain't," and I holstered my shooter. "What's more, I think I'm in the wrong damn business." I pulled some more dodgers out of my pockets and throwed them on the floor. Then I turned and walked away over to the bar. "Give me a bottle of brown whiskey," I said to the barkeep, and he put it and a shot glass on the bar, and I paid him for it. Then the man standing right next to me let out a hooraw laugh, which I took to be aimed at me for backing down from old Applesauce. I picked up my whiskey bottle by its long neck and bashed that son of a bitch across the side of the head with it. Ordinarily I'd call that a shameful waste of good drink, but right then I thought it was worth it. He dropped to the floor like he'd been killed. Applesauce laughed, and I left the bar. Incidentally, I heard some months later that they'd caught up with old Applesauce and stretched his neck over in Arkansas. I felt kind of sorry to hear that he had came to that sad end.

So anyhow, now I guess you can see at least a little bit what I mean when I say that I was fairly snuffy when I first showed up in Asininity. I wasn't no one to be messing around with, that's for sure. And as I said before, Asininity was a wild-ass town in them rough old days. It was truly a fit place for such as I was then. The town had six saloons, all of which was also gambling houses and whorehouses, one general store, one barbershop, a bank, one farm implements store, a combined blacksmith's shop and livery stable, one café, if you could call it that, one lawyer's office, a telegraph office and stage depot all in one room, and one church, which was nondenominational. The preacher had left town, though, and no one knew where he had gone to.

That day I first come into Asininity, back in '79, I had been on the trail for a good long spell. I was hot and dusty and dry, and I wanted a drink worse than I can ever recall wanting one before or since. I hauled up and stopped at the first saloon I come to. It was called Harvey's Hooch House, and I never did find out who the hell Harvey was, but right then I didn't care a damn. I just wanted me a drink of brown whiskey real bad, was all. Well, I went inside that place and up to the bar and had me one, and after I'd had it, I wanted some more.

Well, the next thing I knowed, it was midmorning the next day, and I had just woke up laying in the hot sun out

Robert J. Conley

in the alley back behind the Hooch House with the god-damnedest hellacious skull-pounding headache I ever had, and a right queasy stomach too. My guns, my boots, my hat, and all of my money was gone. I couldn't figure out what to do about my predicament, and even if I could have figured something, I hurt too damn bad to do it, so I just looked around for some shade, crawled into it, and went back to sleep. I figured there would be time enough later on to hunt for the lowlife son of a bitch that had took unfair advantage of me and robbed me in my helpless condition.

Sometime that afternoon, I come awake again. This time I went ahead and struggled on up to my feet. I still felt bad, and my legs was wobbly, but I was awake and stuck with it, so I started to hobbling along slow and easy on my stocking feet back toward the front side of the saloon.

The main street—well, really it was the only street and still is—but anyhow, it was still busy and noisy. There was a fistfight going on out in front of Harvey's Hooch House, and down at the far end of the street, someone was shooting off a gun. I don't know if he was shooting at anything or anyone or not. I wasn't interested and didn't try to find out. I was too busy dodging all the horses and wagons and pedestrians and the nearby fistfight and whatever, and looking out not to step in any fresh horseshit because of my lack of boots, to care about much of anything else, except, of course, my own pilfered belongings, which I was now on the lookout for.

I was a little bit surprised when I found my old horse still tied to a hitch rail there in front of the saloon right where I had left him the evening before, and his saddle was still on his back. The saddlebags was even still there and the blanket roll still tied on behind the saddle. So even though I didn't have no money, nor boots, nor hat, nor guns, I had a horse, a saddle, some blankets, clean socks and a clean shirt, and a few boxes of bullets.

I felt a little guilty at not having boarded my old horse proper-like before tending to my own needs, especially since he had wound up with so long a wait out there at that rail, but I never really intended it that way, and besides,

18

that was all in the past. There wasn't nothing I could do about it then, and he wouldn't have understood no apology if I had tried to give him one. So I just unwrapped the reins and led him down the street to the livery. All along the way, folks was laughing at me, but I just tried to ignore them and endure the humiliation, because I knowed that I wasn't in no condition to get myself into a fight of any kind.

I sold my horse and saddle and saddlebags and even my blankets and bullets to the man in the livery stable. It was old Porkbarrel Stark, and he's still down there, the cheap old son of a bitch. He give me only half of what all that stuff was worth, but I wasn't in no position to argue with him, so I took it and glad, too. All I kept was my clean shirt and socks. I put on the clean shirt and throwed the other one over a rail there at the stable.

"Hell, you might as well take that, too," I said.

Stark just shrugged. He didn't say nothing, and I shoved the clean socks into my pocket along with the money old Stark had give me. I didn't see no sense in putting on clean socks and ruining them too right away by walking around in them without no boots, especially when they was my last only pair. The ones I was wearing was done ruined, so they didn't count, and I figured I couldn't hurt them no more than they already was.

I found the hash house, Maudie's it was, and et a plateful of greasy hash. It made me feel a little better. I've always found that a good greasy meal after a drunk from the night before would go a long ways toward healing the soul. Then I went back over to Harvey's Hooch House and went on inside and just walked right up to the bar like there wasn't nothing wrong at all. I could hear people laughing all the way behind me, but I just gritted my teeth and looked straight ahead.

"Whiskey," I said.

The bartender poured me a shot, and I paid him. It was old Aubrey Waldrip, although, of course, I didn't know that at the time. I downed the shot all in one gulp, and then I really did feel some better. Goddamn, it felt good going down and then settling in my guts. "One more time," I said, and old Aubrey poured me out another drink. I paid him again, but I didn't toss that one down. Instead I just held it in my hand, and I turned around with my back against the bar so that I could sort of study the room. I looked around, casual-like, taking an occasional sip of my whiskey, but what I was really doing was studying on all the hats I could see on anyone's heads. I never did spot my stole hat, though, so I started in looking at boots. It was a little harder to do that casual, but, by God, underneath a table right there in front of me, not six feet away, I seen them. My own damn boots.

I looked away again so as not to let on to the boot rustler that I had spotted him, and then I turned back around and finished off my drink. By then I was feeling total mean and ornery again. I had found the goddamned thief, and in my book he was the lowest kind there is—one who takes a sneaking advantage of a man what's just had his fill of whiskey and is trying to sleep it off and just mind his own business, not bothering another soul in the world.

"Well," I said, kind of loud, "I guess I'll be moving along," and I turned and headed for the door. I walked right past that scurrilous bastard that was wearing my boots and didn't even give him a look, just like I didn't know nothing about it. There was a couple of empty chairs at the next table past him, and as I got up to them, I grabbed one up by the back, turned and raised it way up over my own head, then brought it crashing down on the damned thief's noggin. The poor dumb son of a bitch never knew what hit him. He just kind of slumped like a sack of flour, but I didn't know if he had friends in there or not, so right quick I dropped the chair, and I pulled a six-shooter out of his belt and cocked it. Damned if it wasn't one of my own.

"This thieving son of a bitch is wearing my boots," I said, "and this here is my own Merwin, Hulbert and Company forty-five-caliber, self-extracting revolver. Anybody here got any argument with that?"

Nobody said nothing, so I guessed that they didn't. I dragged the limp and unconscious thief out of his chair and dropped him onto the floor, and with my left hand I managed to pull my boots off his feet. Then I pulled them nasty socks off my feet and throwed them on top of the unconscious thief, right on his face. It wasn't easy to do one-handed while holding a gun on them other boys, but I pulled on my clean socks, which I had there in a pocket, and then I pulled on my boots. I leaned over and got my other revolver out of the thief's belt and stuffed it into the waistband of my trousers. Then I went through his pockets and took out all the cash I could find there. I think that I wound up making a small profit on the deal. Then, my revolver still held ready, I looked hard at the other men still setting quiet at that table.

"Was he wearing a hat when he come in here?" I asked.

One of the men carefully reached up to the back of an empty chair which was setting there between himself and the one on the floor and slowly pulled it out and away from the table. There was my hat in the seat of that chair. I picked it up and put it on my head, and I set it on kind of jaunty-like.

"Is he a friend of yours?" I asked, giving a nod toward the bastard on the floor.

"Well, sort of, I guess," said the man who had showed me my hat.

"Then I sincerely recommend that you check and find out whether or not I killed him," I said, and I turned my back on the bastards and walked out of that place.

I was standing outside on the board sidewalk right after that, trying to decide just what I was going to do with myself next, when a paunchy-gutted, gray-haired bastard in a gray three-piece suit stepped out of the saloon.

"Excuse me, sir," he said.

I looked around and didn't see no one near besides only myself. I wasn't used to being sirred, though.

"You talking to me?" I asked the slick-looking bastard.

"Yes, sir," he said, calling me that again. "Permit me to introduce myself. I'm Randall Peester, attorney at law, and I'm on the town council."

"You mean this dog-ass town has actually got itself a

town council?" I said. I was feeling kind of cocky, I guess, having recovered my property the way I done, and that just after having been made a laughingstock in front of so many strangers, too. Hell, I reckoned that I had showed them all a thing or two, by God.

"Well, yes," Peester said. "It hasn't been very active lately, I'm afraid, but it does exist. It's legal. May I have a word with you?"

"You've done had several," I said, "but feel free. Go on ahead."

"I saw what you did in there to Hook Jackson," he said.

"Is that his name?" I said, not really giving a damn, but it was something to say.

"Yes," Peester said. "He's a bad one. He's had that coming to him for a long time, and I like the way you took care of him. How would you like a job, mister? By the way, what's your name?"

"Barjack," I said. "What's the job?"

And that's just exactly how I come to be hired on as town marshal of Asininity.

Chapter Two

It took me about six whole months, but I finally cleaned up that tough-ass little town. The first very thing I done was I closed down the five rowdiest of the six saloons in town, and then I bought myself a controlling interest in the one remaining. It was Harvey's Hooch House, which I guess I had sort of a sentimental feeling for, and I didn't even change its name, either. And then, whenever the rowdies came in for a good time, I made them check their weapons at the door. I hired me old Happy Bonapart to do nothing but just set there to one side of the front door on a high stool with a shotgun across his knees to sort of intimidate any customers who might otherwise decide to try to get themselves into some kind of mischief. 'Course, I called him a deputy so that his pay would come from the town's coffers and not my own. But then, I thought that was really a sort of a legitimate arrangement. After all, his job was to keep the peace in the Hooch House, and the Hooch House was in town.

Like I said before, Asininity was real peaceful after that for about nine and a half years. Sure, every now and then

Robert J. Conley

I'd have to lock up a drunk for the night or break up a fight. Back in 'eighty-five we had a killing, and I had to gun down the culprit. Got him dead between the shoulder blades as he was trying to leave town. Then there was the time six would-be bad men tried to rob our bank. Not a one of them sorry bastards got out of town alive, and they was all shot so full of holes that they couldn't have been identified even if anyone had give a damn about who they was.

And sure enough, I made myself some enemies over the years, but most of them what didn't wind up in Boot Hill wound up in prison. You can't stay in the law-and-order business without making yourself some enemies, but I wasn't no one to mess around with, and I mean that. But time passes on along, and so do prison terms, and that's where the Bensons come in, and that's what my story is all about. It had all started back in the wild old days, during my first six months on the job.

Back in the rowdy old days, the Bensons had owned themselves a big ranch a few miles west of Asininity. There was five of them then. Some said they was brothers, some said cousins. I never knowed one way or the other, and what's more, I didn't give a good goddamn. But even back in them rugged past times, the Bensons was the worst of a sorry lot of bastards. I think they was Texans originally. If I'm right about that, it sure explains a whole hell of a lot about the way they was. When they come into town, they meant to have themselves a wild rip-snorting time, and after just a few shots of whiskey, they got real mean, all five of them.

One day, they had been in Harvey's Hooch House long enough to have developed a bad case of belligerence when poor old Marvin Cutter somehow or other just rubbed Vance Benson the wrong way. It didn't take much to do that when Vance was drinking. This was back before I had bought into Harvey's and before I had made that rule about no guns being allowed in the place. Anyhow, old Vance just up and shot Marvin dead. Shot him right between the eyes. Vance was a pretty fair hand with a six-gun. And then him and his brothers or cousins commenced to laughing about it real raucous and talking about what a good shot it had been and how poor old Marvin had just fell over stiff like a board and on and on like that.

I was setting right there, and I seen it happen, but I didn't do nothing about it. Not right away. They was all five of them right there together and all armed and feeling mean. I sure ain't no damn fool. I just set there sipping my whiskey, seeming to mind my own business, but actual just waiting for my chance. By and by, Bonnie Boodle got to sidling up to Vance and rubbing on him with her legs and her big titties, and old Vance stood it for a while, but then he couldn't take it no more. He broke out in a cold sweat, and he headed upstairs with her with one arm around her shoulders and that hand hanging down in front between those big titties. I watched them climb the stairs, and then I got up and went outside, casual-like, through the front door like I had drank enough and was leaving to go home and go to bed.

Instead, I walked right on around to the back of the building and climbed the stairs back there that led up to a landing and to an upstairs back door. I opened that door real quiet-like and eased myself into the long hallway that stretched between the two rows of small rooms. Some of the doors was opened and some was not, but I peeked into each room as I come to it. None of the closed doors were locked. They never was. I knowed that already. In two of the rooms I seen half-drunk cowboys trying their best to screw whores, but they was so wrapped up in what they was doing that they never even knowed that I had looked in on them. Most of the rooms was empty. The evening was still young. Finally I come on the right room.

Bonnie was there laid out on her back in the bed with her legs spread wide and kicking around in the air, and old Vance was on top of her, his bare ass looking right at me. Both of them was as naked as jaybirds, except that Vance still had on his boots. I wondered at the time just how he had managed to pull off his britches over them. His gunbelt was hanging on the back of a chair which was standing beside the bed. It was well within his reach. I took a deep breath and then eased my trusty old forty-five out of its holster and tippy-toed into the room.

"Come on, honey," Bonnie was saying.

"Damn it, girlie," Vance said, "you're going to get all you can stand from me before I'm through with you."

Just then I slapped the cold barrel of my Merwin, Hulbert and Company up under the cheeks of old Vance's bare ass, with its muzzle nuzzling up against his balls, and the suddenness of it and the coldness of it along with his own realization of what it was and what it could do to him made him squeeze his ass tight, flinch, and suck in air all at the same time. Then I thumbed back the hammer, and the *click-click* of it was loud as hell in that little room.

"Don't move, Vance," I said, "or I'll blow your balls off."

Well, Bonnie commenced to screaming hysterical-like, but old Vance, he didn't move, and in a minute or two, when she had ran out of breath, Bonnie shut up. Then I made Vance come out of bed backward like a crawdad, and I kept the muzzle of that revolver right down there under his ass. Once he had his feet on the floor and had straightened himself up, then I told him to walk real slow out of the room, down the hall, and on down the stairs.

Well, whenever we made our appearance on that stairway, all the noise in Harvey's Hooch House stopped all at once. It become quieter than a goddamned funeral. Everyone in the place was looking right up at us and staring with their jaws all hanging down and their eyes wide as saucers. There was old Vance, stark naked except for his boots, and me right behind him with a six-gun shoved up his ass. I seen the other Bensons move toward us, menacing-like. Little Red, the youngest and maybe the meanest, but that's a hard call, made a slow move toward his gun.

"You tell them brothers or cousins of yours to keep still," I said to Vance, "or you're going to be ruined for life."

"Don't do nothing, boys," Vance shouted. "This crazy bastard'll blast off my gonads."

When we got down to the bottom of the stairs, I told

Vance to stop and stand still. He did. He was minding me real good.

"You other Bensons drop your guns to the floor," I said, and Vance told them to by God do it, and they did, and then I made them all strip naked, too, and I marched the five of them just like that right out of the saloon, out into the street and on down to the jail, where I locked them all up together in one cell. Then I went back to the saloon for their guns and clothes. I took all their stuff to the jail house, which was also my office, and I tossed it on the floor in a corner.

"Hey," said Vance, "at least give us our clothes."

"You ain't going nowhere that you need to be dressed up," I said.

"Vance," one of them boys said, "what's gonads?"

Early the next morning I went out and rounded up old Hardass Taylor and some of the other local ranchers who had been complaining to me about losing cattle, and we all rode out to the Benson spread and inspected their herd. We found all the evidence we needed. They was the rustlers, sure enough. Of course, as town marshal, I didn't have no jurisdiction out there, so I told Hardass to send one of his cowboys to ride the thirty miles over to the county seat and fetch out the sheriff, old Dick Custer. Old Dick claimed to be an ex–army scout and a buffalo hunter, but I never did believe that about him. He also claimed to be a distant cousin to the dead hero general, but I tended to doubt that damn story too. Old Dick had always been something of a blowhard. But the upshot of all this is that Vance was eventual found guilty of first-degree murder and the other four of cattle rustling, which some thought was worse. Even so, Vance was the only one that was hanged. The others was all just only sent up to the state pen. Oh yeah. O' course, I wound up with the old Benson ranch. And I got it at a hell of damn cheap foreclosure price, too. Old Peester helped me out on that deal. Well, I guess you can see now by my relating of all the foregoing events how come it was the Bensons had it in for me so damn bad.

But you know, one of the funny things about this whole

business is that me and old Bonnie kind of took to each other not long after that, and in just a little while, we become real close, if you know what I mean. Whenever I took over Harvey's Hooch House along with her, I put her in complete charge of the whole gal part of the operation, and I even told her to stop taking on customers personal, because I just wanted to keep her all to my own self. She agreed with that real quick-like too. And while I had the controlling interest in the place, Bonnie owned the rest of it. It turned out to be a pretty damn good partnership—for a while.

So like I already said, it took me about six months to really tame Asininity, but once the job was done, it stayed done, and Asininity become a real peaceful town, a place, like they say, to raise up kids in. We even built us a schoolhouse and hired us a teacher, a skinny little fart with little round glasses with real thick lenses in them. His name was Harrison Dingle, and he was from somewhere back east. I forget just where. Some sissy place like Vermont or something. As time went on, I got older, of course, and a little slower, and put on some weight, but hell, that didn't matter none. It's just the natural course of things, and besides, I had the Hooch House and I had Bonnie.

Then I took and hired me a regular deputy, not just someone to watch over things in the saloon: old Texas Jack Dooly. I guess maybe he was really from Texas, but I never did believe it,'cause he was a pretty nice fellow. He was just a kid, and anyhow, I think he thought it made him seem tougher somehow to be called by that Texas name. But really, the town had become so tame by then that it just wasn't no work at all being marshal. I put most of my energies into running Harvey's Hooch House, and I just kind of left old Texas to watch the streets for me. It got to where if some old boy was fixing to cause any real trouble, either me or old Texas would just plain intimidate the son of a bitch into changing his mind.

We did have us another hanging one time during them relatively peaceful years, but that was only just because old Whiskey Nose Mooney got so drunk that he made a full confession to a murder he done years before. He didn't really think that he was making a confession. He was just talking drunk talk, but what he told was that some years ago, he had got drunk and beat the preacher to death. Then he said he had throwed the body down a well out at the abandoned Woodward homestead. Well, we went out there and looked, and sure enough, we fished what was left of that preacher out of the well. I arrested old Whiskey Nose, and he was right perplexed by my unfriendly action, but I had to take him over to the county seat and turn him over to old Dick Custer. They had a trial over there and eventual hanged old Whiskey Nose. Asininity looked like a damn ghost town for a while. Everyone was over to the county seat to watch the show.

It was like that in Asininity. Not much going on. But then we heard that them goddamned Bensons was out of the pen. At first that didn't worry me too much, because I had done handled them once before, and that when there had been five of them to contend with, not just only four. Besides, I figured they'd likely had just about enough of me the first time around. Then that message come over the wire. Little Herman Simpson brung it to me in the Hooch House.

"This just come in for you, Marshal Barjack," he said, looking timid as hell and holding that piece of paper out toward me, his hand a-shaking.

"Well, hell, Simp," I said, "let me have the goddamn thing."

I jerked it out of the little sissy's trembling hand and read it. There wasn't no words in it that I couldn't handle all right. Here's what it said:

BARJACK
WE'LL BE ON THE STREET OF ASS TOWN
AT HIGH NOON AUG 15. YOU BE THERE TOO.
BENSONS

That was all it said.

Chapter Three

Well, hell, the word was all over the whole goddamn town in just no time at all. And I do mean all over. There was a few old farts setting there at the table with me when I first got the news, and so, of course, they knowed all about it right away, and then I guess old sissy Simpson went out and spread the word around town some more. He ain't supposed to do that, of course, but then there just ain't no sense of decorum in Asininity. Never was. Anyhow, everyone in town knowed about it real quick-like for sure.

I played it like a real cool head, of course. Hell, I couldn't let on like I was skeered of the goddamned Bensons, and besides, everyone knowed how I had took care of them so slick the last time. It hadn't been no trouble at all. 'Course, deep down I knowed that I wouldn't be able to sneak up on one of them again the way I had done before, with his bare ass facing me and his balls hanging down so vulnerable and all that. But I didn't say nothing about it. I just hitched my pants and went over to the bar where Bonnie was just standing there and sipping on a glass of her favorite hooch, and I grabbed her by the arm.

"Let's go upstairs, darlin'," I said.

"Now?" she said.

"Right now, goddamn it," I said.

"But it's only two o'clock in the afternoon, sweetie," she said in that whiney, nasally little voice of hers. For such a hefty broad as she was, she sure had a little snivelly voice. I always thought that was her worst characteristic, but then, I had never took interest in her in the first place for her voice.

"I know precisely what goddamn time of the day it is," I said, and I give a little tug on her arm. "Come on, now. Let's go."

"Well, all right, sweetie pants," she said, smiling at me the way she always done whenever we was fixing to make us some whoopie. She picked up her glass and walked with me on over to the stairs. Everyone in Harvey's was looking at us then. Maybe because I was being so bold and casual in the face of the hard news I had just received, or maybe because I was taking Bonnie upstairs for a romp in the middle of the day, or maybe just because they thought I'd be dead the next time they seen me. I ain't sure. Anyhow Bonnie looked back over her shoulder and give them all a broad grin, and then we walked on up the stairs and went into Bonnie's bedroom and shut the door.

I tossed my dusty old black hat onto a hook on the hat rack and wiped the sweat off my forehead with my shirt-sleeve. "Goddamn," I said. "I sure ain't ready for this."

"Then why'd you bring me up here?" Bonnie said.

"Not that, Bonnie," I said. "I mean, I ain't ready for the Bensons to come back to town gunning for me. That's what I mean."

"Oh," she said. "Well, you handled them before, baby. You won't have no trouble with them. Come on, honey, let's go."

"Damn it, Bonnie," I said, "you know better than anyone else just how it was I got them Bensons rounded up in jail that other time. I sure as hell can't set up a situation like that. Or could I?" I give old Bonnie a look and thought about it for a couple of seconds. "Naw," I said, "it wouldn't

31

never work like that again. And anyhow I was younger then, too, and a damn site crazier. And hell, I didn't have a damn thing in the world to lose in them days. I do have now, and I sure don't want to lose it."

Bonnie moved in close and put an arm around my neck. Just one arm, because she was still holding her drink in her other hand. She squashed her huge tits against my chest and looked up at me with her big blue eyes, which was surrounded by thick paint.

"You mean me?" she said through her nose.

"Well, yeah," I said. "Sure. You too. You and Harvey's and my marshaling job. I got a lot to lose here now. Hell, I got that ranch out there too."

"That old place?" she said. "You don't do nothing with it."

"But I could," I said, "and I mean to one of these days. Hell, if I was to take me a few sticks of dynamite out there and blow that plugged-up creek bed in order to get me some good water flowing, I could run a good-sized herd out there."

I had said all that before and never even come close to doing a damn thing about it. I think I told you already that I done some cowboying work when I was younger. I didn't care nothing about becoming no working cowhand, but the thought of being a big-shit rancher wasn't too bad. If I was to do that, hell, I'd just hire me some old cowboys to do all the work. But that former Benson spread wasn't worth a shit without plenty of good flowing water. That issue had never mattered much to the Bensons,'cause they never run a regular herd out there. They would just steal themselfs a few head of cattle or horses, whatever they could get away with real easy, run them over to their own ranch and hold them there just long enough to make a deal for them somewheres else, then get rid of them right quick.

"Aw, Barjack," she said, cocking her head and giving me one of them kind of looks, "I can't hardly see you working no cows."

"I've done it before," I said, defending my honor somewhat. "I know how, and I can do it agin, if I take a mind to. But damn it all, that ain't what's on my mind. I'm worrying about them Bensons coming back here to get even with me for what I done to them that time."

"Sweetheart," Bonnie said, "quit worrying," and she put her glass down on the table there beside us and then run her hand up into my crotch. I give a little jump. I couldn't help myself. "Remember when that gang of bank robbers come into town to rob our bank?"

"Hell, yes, I recall that, but—"

"You wiped them out," she said. "All six of them. You didn't have no trouble at all with them."

"Hell," I said, "I had the whole damned town behind me on that one. Leastways, everyone who had money in the bank."

"And now," she said, "you've got Texas Jack and Happy both to side you. What the hell're you worrying about?"

She rubbed some more between my legs, and I swear I did quit worrying about the Bensons. I reached around her with both my hands and squeezed her ass real good, and then we give each other a big, slobbering kiss. She started in to pulling me toward the bed, and I remembered the way I had got old Vance Benson, and I broke loose from her real quick and locked the door and tested it to make sure it was real secure. Then I stripped off my clothes real fast and jumped in under the sheets with her. Hell, I didn't care if it was the middle of the day. We had us a real good time.

When we was all done with that, I decided that I had better start to get serious. I needed to make my plans and get myself ready for the arrival of the Bensons. I knowed that I couldn't take on the whole damn batch of them by my lonesome, not and come out of the fracas alive. I got dressed and strapped on my old hog leg, went downstairs and out the front door, and walked on over to my marshaling office. Texas Jack Dooly was just setting there behind the desk with his feet all propped up, and with the Bensons nagging away on my mind, I all of a sudden noticed just how much of a kid he looked to be. I wished right then that he had been at least a few years older and considerable more experienced.

"Howdy, Marshal Barjack," he said, and he smiled real wide, the way no one but a damn stupid kid can smile. It near made me sick to my guts.

I didn't say nothing, though. I just walked on over to the gun cabinet and unlocked the drawer. I pulled out a left-hand six-gun and holster on a belt and strapped that on over the one I was already wearing. I had never had no use for two-gun men before, but just then I felt like an extra shooter on me would be some comfort. I started to shut the drawer, but I thought it over quick-like and pulled out two more revolvers. I checked them to make sure they was all loaded proper, and I tucked them extra two into the waist-band of my trousers.

"Getting all ready for the Bensons, I reckon," Texas said.

"It pays to be ready," I said.

"They ain't coming to town for another week," Texas said.

"Says who?" said I.

"Well, the wire they sent—"

"Exactly," I said, looking him square in the eye and jabbing a finger at his chest. "And who sent the wire? They did."

"Oh," said Texas, like he finally seen the light. "I get it. They might've lied in that wire. They might come on in here early trying to take you by surprise."

"Now you're getting smart, boy," I said. "If you live long enough and keep on a-listening to me, maybe you'll get to be real smart. Not just smart-ass."

"Aw, Marshal—"

"Never mind all that," I said. "Check every one of these rifles and shotguns here. Make sure they're clean and working and loaded to full capacity."

Texas dropped his feet down heavy to the floor and stood up. "Well, I'll be ding-dong damn," he said. He walked over to the gun cabinet to do what I'd told him to do. "You really are a-scared of them Bensons, ain't you?" he said.

"You goddamned right I am, you silly little bastard," I

said. "I'm scared, and if you've got a brain rattling around in your head somewhere, which I doubt, you will be too. There's four of them bastards coming, and they mean to kill me. That means they'll kill anyone else who gets in their way, and that means you. They might come in on the fifteenth like they said, but they might come in early to try to catch me off guard, or they might even wait around a spell and come in late. Let me sweat it out a little. They might come in all four at once with guns a-blazing, or they might sneak in one at a time just intending to back-shoot me.

"Let me tell you something, kid. There ain't a man alive I'm scared to take on face-to-face, but when four big mean bastards come at me all at once with intent to do some serious killing on me, that's a whole different damn deal. And it don't even take a big mean man to kill someone if all he does is he just sneaks up and shoots him in the back. Hell, anyone who can pull a trigger can do that."

Texas had took a shotgun off the rack to inspect, and he hesitated a few seconds, thinking about what I had just told him, I guess. "Yeah," he said. "That's sure something to think about, I reckon."

I turned around and headed out the door. I started toward the Hooch House, and the two extra revolvers I had stuck in my pants was digging into the tops of my thighs real uncomfortable. When I got back into Harvey's I walked over to Happy Bonapart there on his perch. He was just setting there with his shotgun across his knees. I hauled out the two extra revolvers and handed them up to Happy, butt ends first.

"Here. Take these," I said.

"What for, Marshal?" he said.

"Just take them," I said, "and keep them on you at all times."

"Oh, I get it," he said. "You're thinking about when the Bensons comes around."

"Goddamn it," I said. "I wisht everyone would stop reading my mind for me."

Happy took the two shooters and tucked them into his

Robert J. Conley

pants, and I turned and walked off, hoping that they'd poke him in the thighs the way they had done me. I noticed old Harrison Dingle, the schoolteacher, setting at a table all by his lonesome. The only reason I took note of him at all was that I never seen him in there before. He had a cup on the table, and I figured it was just only coffee. He was too much of a sissy to be drinking whiskey like a real man. I stalked on over to the bar. Aubrey Waldrip stepped up with a smile on his face, but it didn't appear to me to be genuine.

"What'll it be, boss?" he asked me. "The usual?"

"You still got that scattergun under the bar?" I asked him.

"Well, yeah," he said. "Sure, but I never even think about it much. Not since you hired Happy to sit there like that."

"Well, think about it, Aubrey," I said. "Get it out and check it."

"Check it?" he said.

"What are you? A goddamned echo?" I said. "Take it out and unload it. Clean it. Reload it. Make sure it's ready for action."

Aubrey leaned across the bar and got right in my face to whisper real low. "The Bensons?" he said.

I heaved a sigh. "Just do what I tell you," I said, and I walked back out the front door. I was feeling somewhat better. I was loaded up with two six-guns, and I had loaded them full, too. Six shots each. To hell with that safety bull about a hammer resting on an empty chamber, I told myself. So I take a chance shooting off a toe. I've got ten of them, and losing one is sure a hell of a lot better than getting shot stone dead by one of the Bensons.

And I had Texas Jack all prepared, with the guns in the office all being checked out and readied for action, and I had Happy over at the Hooch House with extra guns, and Aubrey there at the bar with a shotgun. I figured my best chance when the Bensons come would be to be inside the Hooch House. In fact, it occurred to me that I might ought to move Texas in there too, and then just stay there for good. That is, until the Bensons showed. That way they'd have to attack me on my own ground, and it wouldn't just

36

be me, neither. It would be me and Happy and Texas and Aubrey. Hell, that would be an even fight.

Still, I thought, a fella can real easy get himself killed in an even fight, especially a fair one. I wanted better odds than that. I figured an ambush outside of town would be the best way to deal with the Bensons. Hell, just lay up there in the rocks along the trail with a dozen or so men and just blast the dumb asses right out of their saddles as they come into sight.

I figured I'd talk with Randall Peester, the town councilman who had hired me on in the first place, and give him my plan of action. I'd need more than just me and my two deputies and old Aubrey to carry it through. I found Peester setting behind the desk in his law office. He looked up kind of surprised-like when I barged in, probably because I hardly ever bothered to go see him anymore.

"Barjack," he said. "What a pleasant surprise. What brings you over here?"

"As if you didn't know," I growled.

"What do you mean?" he said, looking somewhat offended. Lawyers really knows how to do that.

"Hell, everyone in town's talking about the goddamned Bensons coming back to town after me for what all I done to them," I said. "Don't try to make out to me that you ain't heard about it."

"Well, yes," the bastard stammered. "I have heard some rumors."

"Rumors, hell," I said. "The bastards sent me a damned telegram. We're coming to town to kill you. That's what it said. The Bensons. That ain't no rumor. That's fact. Here it is right here."

I dug that wire out of my shirt pocket and stuck it right under old Peester's nose.

"Yes, yes, I see," he said. "Well, what do you propose to do about it?"

"There's four of them," I said. "If we just set here and wait for them to get into town, there could be one hell of a gun battle, and innocent folks could get killed. I propose that we get up a twelve-man posse and waylay the sons of bitches out there on the road before they ever get into town."

"You mean, set up an ambush?" Peester said.

"That's just what I mean," I said. "Give them no quarter. Blast them all to hell before they even know what's going on."

"That sounds like deliberate murder to me, Barjack," that old lawyer said. "They haven't broken any laws yet. Not since their release from prison. Not that we know of, anyhow."

"To hell with that," I yelled. I was fast losing my patience with the pettifogging bastard. "We know why they're coming to town. We got their own word for it. We got this right here." I waved the telegram at him again.

"That's not evidence of a crime," he said. "Anyone can send a telegram and put anyone's name on it. It might not even have been the Bensons who sent it."

"Who else would it be?" I shouted.

"I don't know," he said with a shrug. "It could have been anyone. Some crank. Someone with a grudge trying to upset you. You've made more than your share of enemies, you know. Of course, it likely was the Bensons. I agree with you on that. All I'm saying to you is that it is not evidence. In fact, even if we could establish that they did, in fact, send it, they still haven't committed a crime. Not yet."

"Ain't it against the law to threaten murder on a officer of the law?" I said.

"Well, yes, I suppose," Peester said. "But it's not a capital crime."

"What the hell does that mean?" I asked. I was a lawman, but I never knowed no fancy law words.

"One for which the perpetrator can be executed," he said, "and you're talking about executing four men without a trial, when the only crime they may be guilty of is not even a capital crime."

"Now, listen here—"

"No. You wait a minute," he said, interrupting me and making my face burn red. "Let me see that telegram again."

Hoping that his slick lawyer's mind had just come up with some angle for me, I handed him the wire.

"There's no threat here," he said. "It just says that they're coming to town and tells you to be here. That's all it says. No threat. No law has been broken."

"Hell," I said, "everyone knows what they mean by that. They're coming here to kill me. Goddamn it, I marched them all bare-ass nekkid through town. One of them got hisself hanged and the others all spent time in the pen. They lost their damned ranch and their cattle-rustling business. And I don't know if they know this part or not, but, hell, I even got their damned ranch. When you think on it, I cost them a hell of a bundle of money. They're coming here to kill me. Dead. Four of them. And that's all there is to it."

"That's all speculation, Barjack," Peester said. "It may be sound speculation, but it's still speculation."

"So you ain't going to authorize no posse," I said, "not even to save my life?"

"Not to do deliberate killing," he said. "In good conscience, I cannot."

I turned around and stomped to the door, but when I was halfway through it, another thought come into my head. I turned back around to face old Peester again and give it another try.

"What if I was to forget about the killing part and just plan on arresting them?" I said.

He looked up at me kind of curious-like. "How?" he said.

"Well," I said, "just the same way as what I already told you. I'll put six men on one side of the road and six on the other. When the Bensons have rode into the trap, I'll call out for them to surrender. That's all."

"And do you think they will?" said Peester. "Just like that?"

"Will what?" I said.

"Surrender," he said.

"Hell, there's four of them," I said. "What would you do if you was one of four setting horseback out in the middle of the road, and there was twelve men behind the rocks on both sides of you with Winchesters and Henrys and such trained on you? What would you do?"

"I'd surrender," said Peester, but he didn't say no more. He just set there looking thoughtful.

"The only other thing," I said, "is they'll come riding in here with guns a-blazing. I swear to God, I'm just only thinking about the safety of the town folks, Peester. You included. That's all."

"All right, Barjack," he said finally. "Form up your posse. I'll authorize full pay for each member."

Well, I felt like kicking up my heels when I left that office. I figured all my worries was over. 'Course, I still had things to do. Men to round up and plans to lay. But I knowed that I could do it. It would take a little time, was all. And, of course, I also figured that I could just go right on ahead and carry out my own original plan to just blast the Bensons away. What old Peester didn't know wouldn't hurt his ass a bit. I could just say that whenever I called out for the Bensons to surrender, they had went for their guns, and we didn't have no choice but to return fire. Unfortunately, I would say, they was all killed.

I'd never heard anything about no other Benson kin, so once these four was killed, there shouldn't be no more threats made against me regarding their untimely demises. That would be the end of it, and I figured that was the way it had to be. Hell, if I was to just arrest them, the way old Peester wanted, and then get them sent up again, they'd get out again sooner or later, and then they'd be back after me again. I didn't see no profit in that. No, sir. They had to be killed, all four of them, and the sooner the better.

So I headed back over to the office to tell the plan to Texas Jack and to get him to thinking with me about who all we could get to fill up the twelve-man posse I was planning. They would have to be good men with their guns, and reliable. They'd have to have guts enough to blast the hell out of those Bensons with no questions asked, and they would all have to be able to stick to the story that I would give out that the Bensons was the ones that had actual started the shooting.

Fortunately, Asininity was full of them types. They'd do most anything to put a little whiskey and whore money into their jeans, and between me and Texas, I was pretty sure we could come up with eight or nine of them. Nine, I guessed. I probably shouldn't ask old Aubrey to ride out there with us after all. It was one thing to have him keep a shotgun behind the bar for any trouble that might come up in the Hooch House, but really and truly, he was just a bartender and not a lawman or a gunfighter. He probably wouldn't be no good to me out there nohow.

So how it looked was it looked like it would be me and Texas and Happy and then nine more shooters, which we would have to round up. On my way back to the office, I was already running names through my head. I knowed that it wouldn't take much for me and Texas to fill out that list of nine men. Oh, yeah. I noticed Dingle standing out on the sidewalk in front of the Hooch House, and it looked to me like he was a-watching me. I didn't think he was worth giving no more consideration, though.

Chapter Four

"We need us nine good men, Texas," I said as I stepped into my office, slamming the door behind me. Texas Jack looked up from behind the desk where he'd been lounging, the way he most always did when he was supposed to be patrolling the streets.

"What?" he said.

"What's the matter?" I said. "You got dirt in your ears? I said we need to find us nine good men. Get the hell out of my chair."

As Texas moved on out of my way, I walked on around behind my own desk, which, I admit, I spent very little time at anymore, and I set down there in my own chair, which was still warm from where old Texas's ass had just spent so much time. I reckoned that he pretty much kept it warm that way. I opened a desk drawer and pulled out a piece of paper, tossing it across the desk at Texas. He set down there in the wood chair on the visitor's side of the desk.

"You write down the names," I said, and I pitched him a pencil.

"What names?" he said, and he stuck the lead end of the pencil in his mouth.

"The names we come up with while we're talking here," I said. "We got to make up a list of names for a twelve-man posse. There's already me and you and Happy. Put them names down."

"We know who we are," he said.

"Just write down our three names," I said, "with mine at the top of the list. When you run a legitimate office like this, you got to keep good records. Ain't I learned you that much yet?"

Texas wrote down our names, but while he was writing, he looked like he was spending time at hard labor. I never did ask him, 'cause I never figured it was none of my business, but I reckoned that he had never had too much schooling. That didn't bother me none, 'cause, as you already know, I never did neither, having ran off from home at thirteen or so. Even before that, I wasn't never in school much. I was out on the streets trying to hustle a buck. Anyhow, when Texas finally finished writing down them first three names, he leaned back in his chair and blew out a whiff of air, like he'd just finished himself up a real chore.

"Now," I said, "what about old Gar Lowry?"

"For what?" said Texas.

"For the list, dumb ass," I said. "For the posse. What the hell are we talking about here, anyhow?"

"Oh, yeah," he said. "Well, I don't know about Gar."

"Gar's a good man with a gun," I said.

"He was until the other day," said Texas. "His horse stepped on his right hand. Crunched it up a little."

"Can he shoot with his left?" I asked.

"He can't do nothing with his left hand," said Texas.

Well, that did it for old Gar. I reached into my brain for the next name I had already thought of. "Fin Brackett?" I said.

"I don't reckon so," Texas said. "Fin run off with his neighbor's wife. You know? Old Gap Tooth Harman? Fin run off with old Tootie. Gap Tooth don't know where the hell they've gone to. Hey, Gap Tooth can shoot. And he's real pissed off just now on account of Fin and Tootie. He ought to be in just the right mood to do some shooting."

"Write his name down there," I said. So we had four names on the list. Just eight more would do it. I scratched my head. "Who else?" I said. "Who can you think of?"

Texas really wrinkled up his face, and it come to me then that thinking was even harder work for him than writing was. I decided that I was going to have to help him out some more. "What about them two dirt farmers out along the river?" I said. "They're always needing money. This deal would sure help them out, all right. They'll get paid regular wages all the while the posse's formed up. What are their names?"

"Old Scratchy Henderson and the Dutchman?" Texas said. "Is that the ones you mean?"

"Yeah," I said. "Them two. Write their names down. Hurry up."

Well, that brung us up to six. We was halfway there. Then I reminded Texas of old Hardass Taylor's ranch crew, and Texas come up with Shorty Joe, Ten-Gallon Ratliff, Remuda Jones, and a cowboy known only as Chicago. 'Course, Hardass didn't like me worth a damn. He said that he didn't have no use for a man what would let good ranchland go to hell the way I done with that Benson place. I think that he wanted the place himself, though, really. It did lay just right up against his. Anyhow, if we could get them four boys of his, that made ten, and I guess I could have stopped there. That would be five on each side of the road. Ten against four, and the ten set up in ambush. That was pretty fair odds, but I was dead set on having my twelve men, so I kept on thinking and told Texas to do the same. Pretty soon I got to feeling like thinking really was as hard as old Texas made it look. We just couldn't come up with two more names.

"Well," I said finally, standing up and moving out from behind my desk, "keep thinking on it. I will, too. I'm going on over to the Hooch House, and I'll come back here and see you a little later to finish up this list."

I knowed that in order to really ease my mind I had to

get that list finished up and then get them nine men committed to the job, but I'd had about as much of that thinking and listing as I could take for the time being, and I needed a shot or two of good brown whiskey. I hadn't no more than got out the door when Texas was back in my chair, his feet back up on the desk. I seen him through the window as I walked by. Well, hell, I thought, maybe he can think better in that posture.

When I stepped back into the Hooch House little foppy Dingle was setting there alone again, and I seen this time that he had a notebook in front of him, and he was writing in it. There was several other customers in there all having a pretty good time, but they all shut up and turned real somber-like when I walked in. It pissed me off. I walked up to the bar and then turned to face the house.

"It ain't time for my goddamned funeral yet," I said. Then I turned back around, and Aubrey had hustled over to see what I wanted. "Brown whiskey," I said. He poured me a shot, and I downed it. "Get me a bigger glass," I said, and he did, and I poured it about half full. Just then two strangers walked in. They was both big and mean looking, and they was both wearing six-guns. I stiffened up just a bit, wondering if they was going to mean trouble. Happy, setting on his perch there beside the front door, spoke up.

"Howdy, strangers," he said. "Welcome to Harvey's Hooch House. Check your guns here at the door with me before you go in any farther." The strangers both give him looks that was kind of questioning-like. "It's a rule here," he added, and his shotgun was laying across his knees casual-like, but it was aimed generally in the direction of them two toughs. It was cocked, too, and old Happy's finger was on the trigger.

"No man has ever got my gun off of me," said the bigger of the two. "I don't aim to let you be the first."

"Then I guess you can just move on along," said Happy.

"Where's another saloon?" said the other of the two.

"Thirty miles to the county seat," Happy said.

"You mean," said the big'un, "that we can't get us a drink in this one-horse town without taking off our guns?"

"That's about the size of it," said Happy.

The other one pointed a finger toward me, standing where I was over at the bar. "He's wearing two guns," he said.

"He's the town marshal," said Happy, "and he owns this here saloon. I reckon he can do whatever he wants to do. Well, boys, what's it going to be?"

The two drifters started backing off from Happy and spreading themselves apart at the same time. The big one was looking at Happy and his shotgun. The other one was looking in my direction.

"Aubrey," I said, and Aubrey come up with that shotgun from behind the bar. He leveled it at the smaller of the two. Happy raised his gun on up and covered the big one. They both stood still, and then the big one spoke up.

"Hell, Snuff," he said. "Let's get out of this crappy place. The whiskey's probably watered anyhow."

"You should've said that in the first place," I spoke up, pulling out my Merwin and Hulbert Company revolver and walking toward the one nearest to me. "You could have rode out of town real peaceful. Now you're going to jail."

"Going to jail?" said the one called Snuff. "What the hell for? We ain't done nothing."

I moved in close to him, still holding my Merwin and Hulbert on him. Aubrey had his shotgun leveled at him too. I slipped the revolver out of the drifter's holster and tucked it in my own waistband. Then I stepped over to his traveling buddy and relieved him of his weapon.

"You bastards threatened an officer of the law," I said, "and what's worse, you slandered my good whiskey. Happy, jump down off that there perch of yours for a bit and help me walk these old boys on over to the jailhouse."

As we walked them drifters out the door, I could see Dingle writing real fast and furious. I remember thinking in passing what a silly little fart he was.

When we had the two strangers locked securely in a cell, and Happy had went back to his perch at Harvey's, I sent Texas out to walk the streets. I wanted to be alone with the two drifters for just a bit. I had me an idea. I sat down at my desk and propped my feet up, just the way old Texas did. Snuff and the other one could see me real good from where they was in their cell. I tuck myself out a cigar, tuck my time getting it lit, and pretended to be just setting there and relaxing. The prisoners was muttering low back and forth to each other in their cell. Finally I snuffed out my smoke and stood up. I walked over to the cell.

"What's your names, boys?" I said. "Besides just Snuff."

"I'm Snuff Gardner," said Snuff, his head hanging down.

"Dusty Rhodes," said the other one. Neither one of them would look at me, and I could see they was on a real slow boil. That was the way I'd planned it, throwing them in jail like I done for practical nothing.

"Where'd you boys ride into town from?" I asked them.

"Kansas way," said Dusty.

"Down near Wichita," Snuff added.

"Why'd you leave out of there?" I said.

"Wasn't no work," Snuff told me.

"You come up this way looking for work?" I said.

"Yeah."

"You cowhands?" I asked.

"Yeah."

"Well," I said, "there ain't much cowboying work in these parts either. Nor much of any other kind. You boys just wasted a long ride and then got yourselfs throwed in the pokey to boot. All for nothing, it looks like."

"Let us out of here, Marshal," said Snuff, a-whining some. "We'll just ride on out of this damn town, and you'll never see us again. I promise you."

"Me too," Dusty added. "Besides, there wasn't really no harm done. Can't you just let us go?"

"No, boys" I said. "Sorry, but I can't do that. Once a man's been arrested and throwed in jail, there ain't nothing I can do about it no more. It's out of my hands. From there on, it's up to the judge and jury."

"You mean you're going to put us on trial?" Snuff said, kind of unbelieving-like. "Just for sassing you?"

"Can't we just pay a fine or something?" Dusty asked.

"Well, there might just be one way out of this mess for you," I said, acting like I was thinking real hard on it. "Course, it could mean a little trouble. You'd have to be pretty tough eggs."

"What are you talking about?" Dusty asked.

"I got a problem coming my way," I said, "and I need a twelve-man posse. I just got ten. I need two more good men I can count on."

The two drifters looked at each other and didn't say nothing. They was trying to figure my angle, I guess. I decided to press on.

"You'd get out of jail," I said, "and you'd be able to wear your guns around town—even in Harvey's Hooch House. If you was to agree, I'd let you out of that cell right now, give you back your guns, and put you right on the payroll. Right now. Hell, I'd even buy your first drink over in the Hooch House. You'd be out of jail like you want, and you'd have jobs. You said you was looking for jobs."

"What do you say, Dusty?" Snuff said, talking low.

"You got yourself a deal, Marshal," said Dusty. "Unlock this damn door."

"I got to be able to count on you, now," I said.

"You can," said Snuff. "Whenever we sign on with a man, we stick by him."

"You just tell us where to be and we'll be right there on the spot," said Dusty. "Now, open this door. I sure do need that whiskey."

I unlocked the door and swung it wide open.

"Name's Barjack," I said. I walked over to the desk and picked up their guns, and them two was just a step behind me. I turned around and handed the guns to them. "Let's go get that drink," I said.

Out on the sidewalk we met old Texas headed back to the office. I stopped him and introduced him to my two latest recruits. "Write their names down on the list," I said, and then I took the new boys on over to the Hooch House and bought them each a drink. After that they was on their own, I told them. Dingle was still setting there and writing.

I thought about throwing his ass out of the place, but I couldn't come up with no reason for it.

That night I slept pretty good, except for the time me and Bonnie was fooling around with each other. I had my twelve-man posse—well, almost.

August 8

First thing in the morning, after I'd had my breakfast of eggs and ham and taters, I looked up Texas Jack. "I want you to go out riding," I said. "Look up all the men whose names are on our list, and tell them to come right on into town. We got to get busy and gather our forces together."

"You've already got them last two in town," he said.

"Well, dummy," I said, "then you ain't got to go out and gather them in, do you?"

"No," he said, "I guess not. What about Happy?"

"Forget about Happy," I said. "Ride out and get them farmers and cowboys that's on our list."

Sometimes that boy most nearly exasperated the hell out of me, he was so damn dumb. I don't think I ever was that dumb, not even when I was thirteen years old and still snotty nosed back when I beat up that Irish kid in Manhattan. Hell, I wouldn't have done took him on in the first place if I'd knowed who the hell he was. I wasn't that dumb. Not even then. Anyhow, old Texas turned and started to walk away, but then he whirled around to face me once again with another damn question.

"Who's going to patrol the street today?" he asked me, but I knowed that he was just looking for an excuse to hang around town. He just wanted to set all day long with his feet stuck up on my desk.

"I reckon the street'll still be here when you get back," I said. "Most days you spend more time with your feet on my desk than with them pounding out on the street anyhow. Now, get going."

"When do you want them in town?" he asked.

"Right now," I said, and I raised my voice up pretty

good, so that he never said nothing else. He just headed straight on over to old Porkbarrel's livery stable. I stood right there and watched until I seen him ride clean on out of town. Then I tuck myself down to the Hooch House for some more coffee. Old Stinky Poston was already in there, drinking the cheapest rotgut whiskey I had to sell, and there was my two drifters standing at the bar having their morning coffee. Dingle was there, like he hadn't moved at all since the last time I seen him. He was starting in to get on my nerves, so I walked over there to the table where he was setting.

"Dingle," I said, "ain't you supposed to be teaching school?"

"School starts next month," he said.

"Oh," I said, and I turned away from him and walked over beside the drifters and told Aubrey to pour me out a cup.

"Set down, boys?" I said. They joined me at a nearby table, and we all slurped our coffee for a spell without saying nothing. Once or twice I caught Dingle looking at me, but each time he looked back down to his notebook real quick and commenced to writing again. Finally old Dusty broke the silence there at our table.

"Are we for sure on the payroll now, Marshal?" he asked me.

"I told you that yesterday," I said.

"Well, just what is it that we're supposed to be doing?" he said.

"You're doing it right now," I said. "Just hang around here and be handy for whenever I want you. That's all."

Snuff took a slurp of coffee and put the cup down. Then he leaned across the table so's he could speak low to me. "We going to have to kill someone?" he asked me.

"I'll tell you all about it soon as the rest of my posse gets into town," I said.

Right then Dusty let it out that the two of them was some broke. After I had bought them each a drink the night before, they had spent the rest of what they had in their pockets on my booze. They hadn't had nothing to eat since then.

At first I told them that they should have stayed in jail a little longer. They'd have got free meals that way. They didn't seem to see no humor in that, so I give them each an advance on their salaries so they could go eat. I sent them on over to Maudie's and told them to stick close around town.

Well, the rest of the day was pretty much uneventful, except for Dingle looking at me on the sly and taking notes, but late that evening Texas come back in, and he had all seven of them other fellows along with him. I felt pretty damn good. I had my twelve men.

Chapter Five

August 9

Next morning first thing I gathered up my posse in the marshal's office. I felt real kind of puffed up with us twelve men crowded in there. First thing, I introduced Dusty and Snuff to the rest of the crowd. Then I poured us out twelve shots of good whiskey and passed them all around. When everyone had tossed down his shot, I stood up behind my desk and puffed out my chest, trying at the same time to hold my gut in. I hooked my thumbs in the sleeve holes of my vest.

"Men," I said, "I reckon most of you knows just why I got this group together, but I'm going to tell you all the whole damn thing, just so's everyone will know everything. But before I do, I want to tell you that what I have to say can't go no further. This here is a total secretive organization, and the secrets stay right here amongst the twelve of us. Has every one of you got that concept absolute clear in your heads?"

They all nodded and grunted that they had got it, and so I went on.

"There's four Bensons that's coming to Asininity on the fifteenth, if not sooner," I said. "These Bensons is real mean bastards, the worst there is. Most of you likely remembers them from a few years back. When I cleaned this town up, I put five Bensons in jail. One of them got his neck stretched for murder, and the other four went off to the state pen for a long vacation. Well, they're out now, and they sent word that they're coming for me. Now, I don't have to tell you that they won't stop with just me. They'll tear this whole damn town up and kill a few more folks just for good measure. That's just the way they are. Now, hell, I could handle them bastards alone if I had to. I can take care of myself all right. But if they was to come riding into town guns a-blazing, someone else besides just them and me would get hurt—maybe killed. I don't want that to happen. My job is to guard the safety of every citizen in this town, and that's your job too now."

I paused to let all that soak into their heads. I figured a few little white lies never hurt no one. Whenever I considered that they'd had enough cogitating time, I went on some more.

"So here's my plan," I said. "There's a right spot just down the road out of town—the very way they'll come riding in here—right there where the road curves, and it runs smack between two great big piles of boulders. You know the place?"

They all nodded and uh-huhed that they knowed it all right, and I kept talking

"I plan to put six of us in the rocks on one side of the road and six on the other," I said. "Then we'll wait right there till the Bensons comes riding ignorant as hell right into our trap, and as soon as they're between us with no way out, we'll just start blasting away. They'll never know what hit them, and we'll never even have to dodge a bullet. Any questions?"

"Barjack, how do we know when they're coming in?" old Gap Tooth Henderson asked.

"They told me when they was planning to meet me," I said. "I said it once already. You got to pay close attention to everything I say now. It's high noon on the fifteenth. But they might've lied to me about that. They ain't exactly trustworthy. They might try to slip up early on me, so we're going to plant ourselves out there a day early and just wait it out. In the meantime, I want one man out there all the time watching the road, just in case they should come riding along even earlier than that. If he spots them, he'll come running lickety-split right on back in here to get the rest of us."

"I know the place you're talking about, Barjack," said old Gap Tooth. "You want me to ride on out there and take the first watch?"

"Tomorrow morning will be soon enough," I said. "Then you ride on out there. I don't think nobody'll be coming in here to town today."

"Stagecoach ought to be coming in," Shorty Joe said.

"That's right," Texas piped up. "Stage is due today."

"Goddamn it," I said, and I felt like kicking myself in the ass if I could have done it. I hadn't even been thinking about the goddamned stagecoach. Here I had just been figuring that them Bensons would come riding into town on horseback, or at least that would have been their intentions. It never even popped into my thick skull that they might come in on a stage. I thought about all the years that had passed, and I thought that all them years ago, I would've took a long ride horseback, but now that I was near forty years old and a bit heavier, especially in the gut, I wouldn't be so anxious to do such a thing anymore. Well, hell, the Bensons was just as many years older now as what I was, and they had spent them years at hard labor, too.

"What time's it due in?" I asked.

"'Bout two o'clock this afternoon," Texas said. "'Course, that most likely means four or five."

I felt like Texas again, trying hard to think, and it pissed me off at myself. I didn't really think that the bastards would be on that stage, but hell, you never know. I pulled on my mustache and paced the floor a bit. Then I sat down in my big chair behind the desk and rubbed my chin. Finally I looked back up and looked over my twelve-man posse. I noticed that them two drifters was back in a corner a-whispering to each other.

"All right," I said, "listen up now. This here meeting is adjourned, but I want everyone to gather back over at the Hooch House and stay there. Eat. Drink coffee. Play cards. But don't drink no whiskey. You're all on duty, and I need for you to be sober and alert. At two o'clock we'll all meet the damn stage together."

Well, before they left the office, I had Texas pass out rifles, shotguns, and six-guns to them that I considered to be insufficiently armed, and when they walked out of there and headed toward the Hooch House, they looked like a small army. I felt real proud of myself, and only just a little nervous. I felt just a bit like I was thirteen years old again, only this time I was the head of the Five Points Gang. Them damned Bensons was fixing to get a hell of a surprise.

Well, that day dragged on, I can tell you. I spent it, along with my posse, in the Hooch House, with Dingle watching my every move and making notes, and for a while I drank coffee along with the rest of them. I had warned Aubrey not to pour no drinks for any of them. But after a bit I got to craving some whiskey, and I had him pour some on the sly into my coffee cup. It helped some. I also passed a little time upstairs with Bonnie, and then I got me a pretty good idea. I went back down and told the boys that if they wanted to pass part of the day that way, the girls was all available—all except Bonnie, that is. I said that four or five of them could go up at a time, if they was so inclined. That was all the girls that there was anyhow, and besides, I didn't want to be caught by surprise without no protection around me. I told Texas and Happy that they couldn't go upstairs at the same time neither. They was my only two real professional deputies, and I sure wanted one of them downstairs with me all the time.

Well, them two drifters went upstairs right away with Joy Deluxe and Magpie Annie, and then the Dutchman surprised the hell out of me by grabbing onto little old Monkey Nipples. Then Honey Lips latched onto Texas, and he give in to her right easy-like. I was counting my money, all right. Well, sure enough, the boys all spent most of their salaries that day in Harvey's, all except Scratchy, who said that his old woman would kill him dead if he got into any of that stuff, and I congratulated myself on how things was working out. I had needed that big posse to protect my own ass, and I had managed to get the town to pay for it. Now I was sucking most of that town money right on into my own coffers. It seemed like an awful good arrangement to me, and I was thinking on ways to convince the town council that Asininity needed a permanent police force of a dozen or so men. That's what I was still thinking on when two o'clock finally come around. I stood up and hitched my britches.

"All right, goddamn it," I yelled. "Let's go."

I led the way, and we tromped out of there like a troop of soldiers. Dingle hurried along behind us with his notepad and his pencil in his hands.

We heard it coming before we ever seen it. We could hear the pounding of the team that was a-pulling it, and we could hear the thumping and bumping and rattling of the coach as it rolled over the hard prairie road, hitting rocks and bumps and holes in the road, and we could hear the shouts of old Mule Riley as he drove them horses on. He couldn't have drove them that hard all the long way or he'd've killed them. I think he whipped them up like that just before he got into town just to make a show for the folks. Anyhow, we heard it coming, and we waited—real anxious-like. At last it hove into view.

Sure enough, old Mule was up there on the box, and he was popping and cracking that long whip over them horses like billy blazes blue hell, and all the kids on the street was loving it. They was jumping up and down and hollering. Some of them was running to meet the stage. One little fellow had a piece of rope which he was swinging and switching around like he thought it was old Mule's long whip. Up there beside Mule riding shotgun was Hairlip McQueen, and I was struck by how casual he looked up there on that jostling box on wheels with his shotgun laying across his knees. Hell, he looked every bit as comfortable up there as old Happy ever did a-setting on his perch in the Hooch House.

Well, that stage finally pulled up in a great, billowing cloud of choking dust, and the crowd that had gathered there hung back a safe distance from it because of the look of my welcoming committee. As the dust settled a bit, Mule and Hairlip could see why the crowd had hung back. On their left was Happy, Gap Tooth, Scratchy, the Dutchman, Snuff, and Dusty. On the other side of the street was Texas, Shorty Joe, Ten-Gallon, Remuda, Chicago, and me standing just behind them. Every single one of us had two six-guns strapped on, and some had another one or two stuck in their belts. Each one of us was holding either a rifle or a shotgun. We surely must have looked a fearsome bunch.

Well, that stage just set there rocking for a minute or two, trying to settle itself down after its bumpy ride into town, and no one moved. But then old Hairlip set down his gun and climbed down off the box, still looking real casual-like. Our martial presence there didn't seem to bother him none. He waddled straight toward the Hooch House just like everything was normal. The stage door on my side of the road come open then, and all of us tensed up thinking about what we was about to do in case the Bensons come crawling out of there. But they never. There was just one only passenger on that stage, and when she stepped out, I like to fainted.

She was the most beautiful thing I ever seen in my whole entire life. She looked every inch a real lady, a lady the like of which I had never been privileged to meet, considering the level of society I was used to moving around in. Her clothes must have been the latest fashion from Paris or some such damn place, and her skin looked smooth and creamy. My God. I wanted to just fall down in the street and lick the dust off her shoes. It didn't have no business being there. It took every ounce of determination I had, but I pulled myself together, more or less.

"All right, boys," I shouted. "Break it up. False alarm."

My posse mostly headed for the Hooch House, and I stepped boldly out in the street toward the vision of sweetness and light that was just standing there and looking very much out of place. I handed the shotgun I was carrying to Texas as he passed me by on his way to Harvey's and then I took the hat off of my head and did my best to smile pleasant-like. I expect I looked more like a grinning possum, though. I caught myself scratching, and I cut that out real quick and hoped that she hadn't noticed.

"Good afternoon, ma'am," I said. I figured that an ordinary "howdy" just wouldn't do for a lady the likes of her. She smiled back at me real sweet, and I like to have melted down into my boots right then and there. But I kept my cool. "Welcome to Asininity," I said. "I'm the town marshal. Barjack's my name."

"Thank you, Marshal," she said, and oh, her voice was like music, like little tinkling bells, like an angel might talk if they do that. It was real soothing to my ears. I wished that I had dressed myself up somewhat better, but then I thought that I might be killing, not meeting such a creature as what she was. "Were you expecting some trouble here?" she asked me.

"Well, yes, ma'am," I said, knowing that if I'd said otherwise I'd have a hell of a lot of explaining to do about my little army that she seen. "But it's nothing that I can't handle. Nothing for you to worry about none, ma'am. Uh, are you looking for someone?"

"What?" she said.

"What I mean is—is there someone who's supposed to meet you here?" I said.

"No," she said. "No one."

Well, that seemed a downright shame to me, a lovely lady like that getting off the stage alone in a place like Asininity and no one to meet her there. I decided right then and there to do everything I could to make up for that unfortunate circumstance. 'Course, I knew damned well that I wasn't fit for such as she was, but then, I wasn't going to let a little thing like that stop me. No way. Just then old Mule broke up the spell I was in by shouting my name and tossing a big valise down at me. I caught it just in time, and it was heavy enough I like to dropped it, but I hung on.

"What the hell?" I shouted. Then I think that I must have blushed, for I felt my face get real hot. "Excuse me, ma'am," I said, and she just giggled a little, and it sounded like one of them wind chime things in a gentle breeze.

"It's all right," she said.

"The lady's luggage," Mule said.

"Oh," I said, "are you staying in town?" I sure couldn't figure why a lady like her would be stopping in my little town. Oh, Asininity was great for me. I had a hell of a good setup there: a job, my own business, my own private whore, and money in the bank. But it sure wasn't no fit place for a real lady. I had figured that she was just riding through on the stage and I'd never see her again once old Mule had changed horses and loaded up and hauled ass on out of town again.

"Yes," she said. "I'll be stopping for a while in town."

Well, I'll admit to being more than a mite puzzled. She wasn't meeting no one, yet she was planning to stay in town. I stood there like a dumb ass for a minute before I could say anything else.

"Well," I stammered at last, "where will you be putting up, ma'am, if I can be so bold? I mean, I'd be glad to lug your luggage there for you if I knowed where I was to lug it to."

"I thought that I'd get a room in the hotel," she said.

Well, if you can, try to imagine how embarrassed I was at that. Asininity didn't have no hotel. Not a real one. Sometimes if some cowboy or drunk farmer needed a room for the night, we'd let him rent one of the upstairs rooms in the Hooch House, but they wasn't real hotel rooms. They was just rooms for the whores to do their work in. I sure couldn't take a real lady to one of them. My ranch house at the former Benson spread wasn't fit to keep hogs in. The only other thing I had to my name in the way of a place to stay was just my marshaling office with its jail cells and a little back room that I could sleep in and change my clothes in. That sure wouldn't do.

I racked my brain trying to think up some solution to this problem. I couldn't just stand out there in the middle of the street with her, me holding that bag like I was, and I couldn't think of no decent place to take her to. Then I recalled the little house on the edge of town that old skinflint Peester had tried to sell me on more than one occasion. I had told him them times that I just didn't have no use for no cute little house, and as far as I knowed, the little son of a bitch was still just setting there empty. I made up my mind in a flash.

I walked the lady over to my office, apologizing all the way, and I made her as comfortable as I could in there. Then I excused myself, promising to be back in a flash, and I hustled over to Peester's office and made me a fast deal with him. I promised to pay him more than what I wanted to pay, but I was in a hurry and kind of desperate. Then I hurried over to the Hooch House and sent Texas after a horse and buggy, telling him to have it brung right over to my office, and then I set Aubrey and a couple of whores, old Joy Deluxe and Magpie Annie, to fixing up the best steak dinner they could muster. I told them to have it delivered to my new house as soon as it was all done up. Then I almost run back to my office. The lady still looked just as fresh as a prairie flower. I stepped in the door and stood still, whipping the hat off my head.

"Ma'am," I said, "I've found you a decent place to stay, and if you'll allow me, I'll drive you over to it." I glanced out the window and seen the buggy being drove up just then. She stood up and thanked me, and I picked up her heavy bag again and waited while she walked out the door. Porkbarrel climbed down out of the buggy, and I shoved the luggage into his chest.

"Load this," I said. He looked a mite surprised, but he done like I said. Then, before he could say anything more, I said, "Send the bill to my office," and I took the lady's hand and helped her up onto the buggy seat. Oh, the touch of her hand sent strange feelings coursing all through my whole body, and my knees got weak and wobbly, and I feared something fierce that I might just fall smack down right there in the street. I didn't, though. I managed to keep on my feet and walk around to the other side and climb up there to set right beside her. God, I could smell her perfume. Then, as if I was doing just fine, I gathered up the reins, give them a flick, and drove her over to the house I had just bought. Whenever I hauled up there in front of the house, she give me a kind of a questioning look.

"Whose house is this?" she asked me.

"Well, ma'am," I said, thinking that I'd better choose my words real careful-like, "it belongs to me, but I don't live here. It'll all be proper-like. Don't you worry none about that, ma'am."

"What about the rent?" she asked me. "I was expecting, of course, to pay standard hotel rates, but—"

"Oh, please, ma'am," I said, interrupting her. "Don't worry none about that neither. This old house has just been setting here empty. It won't put me out none to have you staying here. In fact, it will be a pleasure and an honor for me to have a lady of your quality staying right here in my house."

"Well," she said, real kind of demure-like, "I just don't know what to say, Marshal—Barjack—except thank you."

I helped her out of the buggy and unlocked the house to let her in. Then I lugged her bag in there for her and give her the key to the front door. I looked around the little house. I'd never been inside it before, but I didn't want to let her in on that information. It looked all right.

"A little dusty," I said. "I'm sorry about that, but I wasn't expecting no guest."

"It's all right," she said. "It will be just fine."

"Are you hungry, ma'am?" I asked her. " 'Cause there ain't no fit place to eat in town, but I can have you a real nice dinner sent over."

"Why, thank you again, Marshal," she said. "I'll accept on one condition."

"Yes, ma'am?" I said.

"That you join me for the meal."

Chapter Six

Well, I was wallering around in hog heaven, I can tell you. I could scarcely believe what had happened to me. Hell, I forgot about old Dingle and his note taking, and I practical forgot all about the goddamned Bensons. 'Course, I didn't really forget about them. A man can't hardly forget that four men's coming to town to kill him, but what I done, I think, is I told myself that they wouldn't likely show up until they had said they would, at high noon on the fifteenth. And even if they was to show up early, I would have my lookout out there on the road, and I had my posse. Twelve of us altogether. I was ready for them bastards. I told myself I could afford to relax a little and enjoy the wonderful good fortune that just came my way.

I told the lady that I'd leave her for a little while and let her get settled in there at the house, but that I'd be back with the dinner, and I thanked her kindly for the sweet invite. Then she told me her name. It was Lillian Fields. I thought that it was the most prettiest name I'd ever heard, and I just kept on saying it to myself over and over as I hustled on back to the Hooch House. I made one of my new posse men take the rig back to old Porkbarrel, and I hustled on into the kitchen which was back behind the bar out of sight. It didn't hardly ever get used, but I sure had need of it then. I yelled at them two whores that was doing the cooking to throw on another steak and some more of whatever else they was cooking up and to hurry up about it. Then I went back out to the bar and had Aubrey pour me a shot. Well, actually it was more than just a shot. I was just sipping at that good whiskey when old Bonnie come stomping up to me.

"What the hell are you up to, Barjack?" she yelled out at me.

"What are you talking about, Bonnie?" I said.

"I seen you driving that woman down the street in that buggy," she said, "and you got Joy and Magpie back there cooking up a steak dinner for two."

"I'm just only welcoming a visitor to town, baby doll," I said. "That's all. She's a lady come to stay a spell, and there ain't no fit place for her to put up and no fit place for the likes of her to eat. So being a town official and all, I thought I'd see that she was took care of proper. Well, once I had done her those little favors, she invited me to partake of the meal with her. I couldn't hardly refuse, now, could I?"

"Are you sure that's all there is to it?" she said.

"That's all," I said, but deep in my heart I was sure as hell hoping that it wouldn't be all. I had been smit by the absolute and pure wonderfulness of Lillian Fields.

"How long's she planning on staying here?" Bonnie asked me.

"Well, now," I said, "I don't rightly know, sweet thing, but I figure only a few days. I'll see if I can find out, though, and I'll let you know."

"Now, Barjack," she said, and her voice was awful shrill, "you better not be planning on slipping around on me. You and me is business partners and more than that, and if I catch you messing with some other woman, I'll kill you. I surely will."

"I know you will, darlin'," I said, "and that's just why I

ain't fixing to do nothing like that, that and because I'm stuck on you."

"Truly?" she said.

"I'm truly stuck on you, sweets," I said, and it was making me sick to be saying it, "so you just calm yourself down and don't be worrying no more. There ain't no woman for me but just only you."

"Well, all right," she said, "but all I can say is that you better be telling me the truth."

Well, Bonnie quit yelling and complaining, but she had a real sour expression set on her face, and it sure didn't help my new opinion of her looks, now that I had met up with Lillian Fields. I was thinking that if things was to develop, so to speak, with Lillian, I'd have to dump old Bonnie. She could find herself someone else or go back to taking on customers like she used to do. That would be up to her. But if I was to have the marvelous opportunity to choose between them two, well, there just wouldn't be no question at all about what my choice would be. No sir. No question at all.

But it wasn't going to be an easy matter dumping that old broad. I knowed that for sure. She had actual meant it real literal-like when she had said that she'd kill me. She was a bad-tempered woman, and when she was riled, she was capable of just about anything. I'd have to be real careful the way I come up with to break apart with her, but I figured that by the time that actual come up, I'd figure out just how to handle it in the best way so as to save my ass.

Well, just about the time I was fixing to lose all my patience and my temper, the dinners was brought out on a big tray with a cover over it, and I sure did wish that it was a fancier setup. But there had never been no fancy restaurant in Asininity, and so there wasn't no fancy restaurant dishes. I made up my mind right then and there to open one up. Since I had shut down five saloons, there was five empty buildings to choose from. 'Course, any one of them would have to be remodeled some, but that wouldn't be no problem. Then I thought that I could take the biggest of the buildings, that would be what had been the old Watering Hole, and I could redo the little rooms upstairs too, and I could have me a respectable hotel, one without no whores in it. But there would be plenty of time to think about that later.

I told Bonnie to tend the bar for a while so Aubrey could go deliver the meal to the house I had bought. 'Course, I didn't tell Bonnie or Aubrey that part of it—that I had bought the house. I just said to deliver it to old Peester's little house on the edge of town. Well, Bonnie went back behind the bar and glared real hard at me, but she didn't say nothing. Then I hurried on over there so that I would arrive before Aubrey did. I knocked on the door real respectable, and right soon Lillian opened it up. The sight of her and the whiff of her sweet perfume that I got like to knocked me over.

"Come in," she said in that pretty little tinkling voice of hers.

"Thank you, ma'am," I said, and I whipped the hat off my head and stepped inside. "The dinner's on the way," I added. Then I saw that she had done wiped off the table and had places set there for the two of us.

"Why, that there looks real nice, ma'am," I said.

"Please call me Lillian," she said. " 'Ma'am' is so formal, and I think we're going to be friends."

"Oh, I surely hope so, ma'am," I said. "I mean, Lillian."

All of a sudden I wished that I had took me a bath and changed my clothes. Standing there in the living room of a real house, and a kind of pretty little house at that, and looking at that fine lady, I felt like a hard-rock miner just crawled out of his hole, and I just had to say something about it to sort of excuse myself.

"I apologize for my appearance, Lillian," I said, "but I've had a right busy day marshaling, you know, and there just ain't been time for cleaning up. I feel bad coming over here to keep you company looking like I do, but—"

"Please don't apologize," she said. "I understand, and besides, you look just fine. You're really quite a handsome man, you know."

Well, I did kind of know that,'cause I had a habit of studying myself in the mirror pretty regular. I was getting some wrinkles in my face, and I looked hard and tough because of the kind of life I'd led. My belly was getting a little paunchy, but still I reckoned that I cut a pretty good figure for a man my age and considering the using I'd had. Still, it was awful nice hearing a fine lady like Lillian say it right to my face.

"Thank you for them kind words," I said, and then I begun to feel just a little uncomfortable,'cause I couldn't think of nothing to talk to a real lady about. I think I just shuffled my feet a little, and then she asked me to set down on a thing she called a love seat. She set on its other end from me, but it was just a short thing, and she wasn't very far away. I was still wondering what I would say to her when I heard a knock on the door. I jumped up.

"That'll be old Aubrey with our dinner," I said, and I just about run over to the door. It was Aubrey all right, looking kind of sullen, and I told him to bring the tray on in and set it on the table. He did that, and then he grumbled his way back out, and I shut the door behind him. I pulled out a chair for Lillian to set down in, and then I set in the other one, and we commenced to eat our steaks and drink our coffee. I wished that the Hooch House had stocked champagne, but up till just that very minute there had never been no call for it. I decided that I would order some in with my next shipment of booze.

I was real careful all through the meal to use my very best manners. Even though I never even thought about them much, I knowed how all right. I put both my elbows on the table, not just the right one. And when I sopped up gravy with my bread, I just kind of daubed at it real genteel-like. I didn't slurp out loud when I drank my coffee neither. Once when I felt a big burp coming on, I just swallowed it down and never made a sound. When we had finished, Lillian started to gather up the dishes to wash them, but I jumped right up and stopped her.

"No, you don't," I said. "I won't have you putting your hands in no dishwater." I didn't like to think of them lovely hands of hers getting wrinkled up from soapy water, so I just stacked them back on the tray and set the cover back over the whole mess. "I'll run them back down to the—to Harvey's here in a while."

"Thank you," she said, and then she suggested that we go back to the love seat and set and talk a spell. She didn't have to say it twice.

"Lillian," I said, "your unexpected but very welcome presence in town has brought some real important things to my attention." Then I told her about my new plans to open up a real respectable hotel and restaurant, so that when respectable folks come through Asininity they'd have a decent place to stay in and to eat at. "And it's all due to your coming into town that I come to think of it at all," I said.

"Why, I think that's it's a wonderful idea," she said. "So entrepreneurial. I didn't know that you were a businessman as well as the town marshal. My word, I'm really impressed."

"Well," I said, "I do own the saloon in town, and the—"

I had started to say the gal business, but I stopped myself just in time. I sure didn't want to bring that subject up to a fine lady.

"And?" she said.

"Well, I meant to say, I own the only saloon in town," I said. "It does me pretty good, and I have me a little ranch over west of here, it needs some attention just now, but I would like to have a more respectable business," and I noticed that that word "respectable" kept popping up in my conversation and in my thoughts. It was something I'd never worried about before.

"You're a very interesting man," she said. "I don't think I've ever met anyone quite like you. I'd love to see your hotel and restaurant when you get it opened."

"Well, now," I said, "just how long do you reckon you might be hanging around these here parts?"

She shrugged, and the movement of her smooth shoulders sent chills through my whole body. It was just all I could do to keep my hands to myself, but I sure didn't want to do nothing to offend her and mess up what I thought I had going with this fine lady. With a whore you can just say, let's do it, and then you get it on, but with a real lady, well, I wasn't for real sure just what you do, but I was pretty damn certain that you just don't just climb on them like that.

"That's hard to say," she said. "It depends on what I find here that I like. I really have no specific plans. There was some—unpleasantness where I used to live, and I just had to get away. Actually, I'm looking for a place to settle."

Oh Lord, I wanted to find some way to encourage her to hang around Asininity, but I sure as hell couldn't think of a goddamned thing to recommend the place. I wondered a bit about the unpleasantness that had drove her away from her former place of residence, and it come to me that maybe some damned cad in the disguise of a gentleman had done her wrong. I wished I knowed where to find him so I could kill him for her. I thought about asking her about the unpleasantness, but I figured that was another one of them things you just don't ask a lady about. Well, the conversation kind of deteriorated after that, and I excused myself the best way I knowed how and went to pick up the tray.

"Will I see you tomorrow?" she asked me, and I think my heart actual fluttered at them sweet words. "I'd like to."

"Well," I said, "do you reckon that maybe I could take you out for a little buggy ride?"

"That would be nice," she said. "About ten in the morning?"

"I'll be here with bells on," I said, and when I left that little house that night I felt like I was walking on the air. I didn't feel no cares nor worries. I didn't think about no Bensons. It was still too early, of course, to read too much into anything she had said or did, but, by God, at least she liked me some, and as for my own self, well, I suddenly realized that something most powerful had happened to me, and it was something that I had never thought would ever happen. I had fell in love. I was in love with Lillian Fields. *Love* was a word that I'd likely never even spoke in my life, and it was never in my thoughts neither. I'd never had it and never wanted it. Never saw no use for it. But it sure popped into my head that night. I was in love. I had caught a most terrible case of it, too.

Back at the Hooch House, I put the tray on the bar and told Aubrey to get me a drink. He poured me a glassful, then took the tray back to the kitchen. Bonnie was setting at a table by herself looking real sour. She stared at me for a little, then got up and walked on over to stand right beside me. She carried her drink along with her.

"Well?" she said.

"Well what?" I said back at her.

"What was you doing over there for so damn long?" she said.

I started to get a little riled up, her talking to me like that, but I held it back. After all, I wasn't yet for sure just how far things might develop between me and Lillian, and if she was to up and leave town on me, well, I didn't want to take no chance on spoiling what I already had going for myself with Bonnie and wind up with nothing. So I knowed that I'd have to kind of string old Bonnie along, just until I knowed for real about me and Lillian. I mean, the pleasures of old Bonnie's flesh was better than no flesh pleasures at all.

"Just only what I told you before," I said. "Nothing more. We ate a meal and we talked some. I asked her how long she'd be hanging around, and she said she wasn't for sure, but I still think it'll be just for a few days is all. There ain't nothing in this town for a lady like her. She's used to high-falutin' things, you know, fancy hotels and restaurants and things like that. Opery houses, probably."

It come into my head just then that I had ought to build us a opery house in Asininity. Hell, the county seat didn't even have no opery house. I figured that would cost a bundle, so I made up my mind not to say nothing about it for a while. I'd get the hotel and restaurant done first and then maybe get my ranching business going. Whenever I had me a big enough bankroll, I'd think again on the opery house. And I didn't bother telling Bonnie that I was planning on establishing something to suit ladies and gentlemen, neither. She'd find out about that soon enough. Well, I drank down about half that glass of whiskey, and the way I was feeling because of my evening with Lillian, with each swaller, old Bonnie begun to look just a little better to me again. I picked up my drink and swung my other arm around her shoulders.

"Let's you and me go upstairs, sweety," I said.

Well, that sure took the sullen pout off her face. She took hold of my arm with both hands and snuggled right up against me and smiled. I guess she must have figured that if I'd been into anything with someone else, surely I wouldn't be in the mood for it with her so damn soon afterward.

"That's more like it, baby doll," she said with a nasally giggle, and we walked together over to the stairs and on up and into her room. Well, I tell you what, I pounded myself against old Bonnie most all that night, but it was Lillian I was thinking about. I just couldn't get Lillian out of my mind. What the hell? I never even tried.

Chapter Seven

August 10

First thing the next morning, I sent old Gap Tooth on out
to the rocks to watch for the Bensons on the road. Then I
had myself a big breakfast over at Maudie's. I was real
hungry after the night I'd had, and I had a big day planned
for myself too. I went back over to the room and told Bonnie to have me a bath drawed, one with real hot water and
lots of soap bubbles. When I had washed myself real good
and sprinkled myself all over with lilac water, I dressed up
in my best suit. I had hardly ever wore it. It was black,
with a vest and a long-tailed coat. I had on a clean white
shirt with ruffles on the chest and the cuffs, and I made
Bonnie tie me up a real nice black necktie. I dusted off my
old black hat, and it didn't look half bad, but I told myself
that I had ought to go out and get me a new one. Then I
shined up my black boots till I thought I'd like to rubbed
them thin. I strapped my two six-shooters on under my
coat, and then I was ready to go.

Bonnie kept eyeing me real suspicious-like, wondering,

I reckon, why I was getting myself so spiffied up. She didn't say nothing, though. Not at first. But when I set my hat on my head and took a long look at myself in the mirror, she finally spoke up.

"Where you going?" she asked me.

"I'm just stepping out for a look around," I said. "That's all."

"Why'd you take a bath?" she said. "And what're you all dressed up like that for?"

"Bonnie," I said, "you're a goddamned suspicious-minded woman. Did it ever occur to you that what all we done together all night long might have just put me in a real good mood and made me feel like getting myself all dandied up like this?"

Well, hell, I don't know if she really bought that line or not, but she didn't say nothing else, and I tripped on down the stairs and walked out the front door a-whistling and a-strutting. I noticed that some of the boys give me real funny looks as I walked by, and Dingle was still writing in his notebook. I ignored them all and just strolled on down to the stable, where I made old Porkbarrel hitch me up the nicest rig he had to the best horse he had, she was an old gray mare, and then I climbed up on the seat and drove on over to pick up Miss Lillian at my new house. I hauled up there in front and walked to the door and give it a knock. Lillian opened it right away. She was ready and waiting, and that made me feel good. I whipped off my hat and give her a good stare. I couldn't hardly believe that each time I looked at her fresh, her wonderful good looks surprised me all over again. She was like an angel from heaven, if there is such a place. She really was.

"Good morning, Marshal," she said.

"Good morning, Lillian," I said. "You don't have to call me Marshal. I'd ruther you just call me plain old Barjack, if you don't mind."

"All right, plain old Barjack," she said, with the most loveliest of smiles on her sweet face, "shall we ride?"

At that she cocked her arm out to the side, and I knowed enough to take it, and I did and walked with her to the buggy. I helped her up onto the seat, and then I walked around to the other side and climbed up there myself. I gathered up the reins and give the horse a flick and a chuck, and we started to roll. I felt like the Emperor of Asininity, I can tell you. Well, I turned that rig around and drove right down through the middle of Asininity, letting everyone see me like that, all snazzy like I was and with that incredible beauty setting right up there beside me. My nose was poked away up high and snooty, too. There wasn't nobody as good as me. There wasn't a goddamned soul alive with as much great good fortune as I had.

Well, I knowed a right nice spot out by the river with a little grove of trees, damn near the only trees for thirty or so miles around. You could set there in the shade and listen to the water as it ran bubbling on down the riverbed. I knowed about it, but I never hardly went out there. That sort of thing just wasn't in my normal nature, but then, neither were the feelings I was experiencing over Lillian Fields. I kind of thought that it was a place she'd take a liking to. The only thing was, I had to drive out beyond the rock where old Gap Tooth was a-standing guard for me. I told myself that it was still a mite early for the goddamned Bensons to come riding into town, and therefore it would be all right. I headed right on out that direction.

"It's very kind of you to drive me," Lillian said. "I don't know what I'd be doing to amuse myself otherwise."

"Oh, it ain't that I'm being kind," I said. "I'm just real proud to have your company. It's giving me great personal pleasure, believe me, it is."

"I'm glad of that," she said. "Thank you."

We drove on then for a while without saying nothing, but it was all right, and then we come to the rocks. When we got closer, I seen Gap Tooth rise up on top of a big boulder over to my left. He was holding his old Henry rifle.

"Hey, Barjack," he called out. "That you a-coming?"

"Course it's me," I said, hauling back on the reins and stopping the rig. "Who'd you think it was? Can't you see me?"

"I never seen you looking like that before," he said.

"What the hell do you know?" I said. Then I realized what I done, and I tipped my hat at Lillian. "Sorry," I said. "I kind of forgot myself there for a minute."

She smiled that coy smile she had and said, "Think no more of it . . . Barjack."

"Well, anyhow," I called up to Gap Tooth, "what would you know about it? You hardly ever get into town to see what I'm looking like anyway."

"Well," he said, "I seen you enough times, I guess, and I never seen you all dressed up like that."

"Never mind about it," I said. "Has the road been clear?"

"I ain't seen a soul till now," Gap Tooth said. "No one riding in or out."

"Well, keep a sharp eye," I told him, and I snapped the reins and drove on. Pretty soon I turned off the road, went on over to the edge of the river, and stopped there. I got down and went around to the other side and helped Lillian out of the buggy. Her step was sure light. I thought I could have picked her up and held her in just one hand.

"This here's the prettiest spot of country for miles around in any direction," I told her. "I just kind of thought you might like to see it."

"It's lovely," she said, and we walked together over close to the water. There was a log laying down there under the trees in the shade, and we set ourselfs down on it. For a little while, we just set there silent, listening to the water babble its way on downstream. "This isn't on your ranch?" she asked me.

"Oh, no, it ain't," I said. "My spread is out that way." I pointed off to the west kind of vague.

"I'd like to see it sometime," she said.

"It's a little far out," I lied to her just a bit, "and besides that, it really ain't a fit place to show just now, especially not to the likes of you. I got me quite a bit of work to do out there, before it'll be ready to show to a real genteel lady, and I been so tied up what with my marshaling job and my business interests in town, I just ain't got around to it. But I mean to. I got to go out there and dynamite a little stream in order to open me up the water supply, and

I need to work on the old house some too, or maybe just tear it down and build me a new one. I ain't decided just yet on that." Of course, I had never really even given it no thought before just that very minute, but I didn't tell her that.

"Barjack," she said, changing the subject on me, "that man back there beside the road—he's working for you?"

"Yeah, well, you might say he's a kind of a special deputy," I said.

"And he's watching the road for you?" she asked.

"Yes," I said. I kind of knowed where she was headed with them questions, but I didn't really want to encourage the conversation going in that direction. I didn't want her to get scared out of town or nothing, so I didn't answer her no more than just exactly what she asked me. I was hoping that she'd change the subject again before I had to tell her too much, but then I never did see that just hoping ever got anyone anywhere. "He's just kind of looking out for someone for me," I added. "Someone I'm expecting."

"And yesterday when the stage arrived in town," she said, "you had a number of armed men on both sides of the street. What kind of trouble are you expecting, Barjack? Please tell me."

Well, I couldn't hardly resist her when she'd put it to me real sweet like that, so I wound up telling her all about the Bensons, what I had done to them and what they was threatening to do to me. 'Course, I left all the ugliest parts out of the story. And I didn't want her to think that there was anything cowardly about me neither, so I used that line about how if I was to just let them ride into town, and if I was to face them then and there for a showdown, well, some innocent folks was likely to get hurt or killed. Women and kids maybe. I said I couldn't have that happen. When I had finished the tale, I told her that I had everything well under control, though, and that it wasn't nothing for her to worry about.

But she was worried. I could see it in her, and it touched me real deep, 'cause I seen that she was worrying for my safety, and that meant that she really did care about me.

Well, I got real bold then, and I reached right over and just laid my rough old hand on top of her real delicate one, and the feel of her soft skin was surely a thrill, and then I looked her right in her big, round eyes.

"Lillian," I said, "I know it's been just only a real short time since we met, but I got to ask you something."

"Yes?" she said, and her voice sounded real little just then.

"Do you think that you could maybe learn to really care for me?" I said. "I mean—really?"

She ducked her head and turned it just a little away, and I could see that she was blushing some. I thought that I had done gone too far, and I was about to come out with some kind of apology when she spoke up first and stopped me just in the nick of time.

"I think I could," she said. "I could. I do. I really do."

"You do?" I said, most afraid to believe what I thought I was hearing. "Already?"

"Already," she said. "Right away. Yesterday afternoon when you drove me over to your house."

"Really?" I asked her.

"Really," she said.

"Do you think that you could—I mean, do you reckon that it might be possible that when I get this Benson mess all cleared up and when I get started in to working on my hotel and restaurant and maybe start in to getting my ranch all fixed up and making it a going concern—well, then do you think that maybe you and me might could . . . get hitched up together?" I said, and I knowed that I was kind of stammering. I had never even tried to talk to a woman that way, much less a real fine lady, and part of me was having a time believing that I was really and truly hearing my own voice saying them words. Hell, I had never before had nothing to do with no woman other than just whores.

"You mean—married?" she said.

"Yes, ma'am—Lillian," I said. "That's just exactly my true meaning. I know it's right bold and forward of me asking you so quick, but I knowed it right away whenever I first laid eyes on you that I was deep down lost in love.

I ain't never been that way before. Not ever."

"Barjack," she said, "I'm very touched by your proposal. It's sweet. But it's so sudden. You've caught me completely by surprise. I—How long would we have to wait?"

I found them last words of hers real encouraging, so I spoke up as fast as I could to answer the question.

"This Benson business will be over with and done for good on the fifteenth," I said. "Maybe sooner. I'll get to work on my new business and on the ranch right away after that."

"You must be doing very well indeed if you can afford to set up a hotel and restaurant," she said. "That's an expensive proposition."

"Well, I'm pretty well fixed," I said, "and it's right that you should know about that too. I wouldn't want you to get yourself into something that you didn't know just what it was. And I'd want you to have the final say on the way the place is dolled up, you know. A woman's ideas is just what's needed to make it real nice and respectable. 'Specially a real lady like yourself."

"Oh, Barjack," she said. "Yes. Yes, I will marry you." And she leaned over and give me a real gentle kiss on the cheek, and I was glad I had shaved that morning. I decided right then that I would have to cultivate myself a new habit of daily bathing and shaving, and I'd have to buy myself a whole bunch of new clothes. That was the least that lovely Lillian deserved from me, and besides that, it would be necessary to suit my new respectable status in town.

A most delightful image come floating into my brain just then, and it was a picture of me in a fancy suit with a black, long-tailed coat and black britches, a gray, striped vest, and a white shirt with ruffled cuffs. I didn't have on no boots, but instead I was wearing shiny black pointy-toed shoes with white spats, and I was strutting along with a walking stick in my hand. It had a gold knob on top. And on my left arm was Lillian, wearing a most beautiful gown straight imported from Paris, and she was carrying a parasol to keep the sun off of her lovely skin. Everyone on the street was stepping out of our way and bowing to us and wishing us a good day. And I figured that was just how it was going to be, just as soon as I had killed those goddamned Bensons.

Chapter Eight

Well, I just couldn't believe my own great good fortune and how everything was just falling right into my lap. I was fixing to become a married man, and not only that, I was going to have probably the finest lady I had ever seen in my whole entire goddamned life for my wife. I was going to open myself a hotel and restaurant and be a respectable businessman and a goddamned rancher. Already I was the town marshal and owned the controlling interest in Harvey's Hooch House with all its liquor, gambling, and gal business. Everything was looking great. Everything was going my way. The only horse apple in the gold street was the imminent arrival of the goddamned Bensons. But I had that covered too. I wasn't going to let that little matter bother me none. I swore that I was not going to let them worthless bastards spoil all the wonderfulness that was happening to me.

But there was still Bonnie to deal with too, and I knowed that I was going to have to face up to that unpleasantness real soon. I had managed to lie to her so far, but now I had actual popped the big question to Lillian, and I was for sure the word would be all over town in a real big hurry, just like the word had got around about the Bensons. I decided to face old Bonnie right then and get it over with. I went into the Hooch House, but Bonnie wasn't nowhere in sight. I figured she was still sacked out from our wild night. I was a little tired myself, but I was all so excited about things that I couldn't have slept on a feather bed. I went on upstairs and opened her door, and there she was, sure enough, all sprawled out there like a big hog in its waller. It come into my mind just then that I had wallered in it with her all night long, but I shoved that thought aside.

I walked on over to the side of the bed and give old Bonnie a hard slap on the ass. She popped up right quick and give a yelp, but when she seen it was me, and all dressed up, too, she give me a smile, but now I thought it was almost ugly compared to the sweet smiles I had been getting from Lillian. I asked myself just how in the world I had made myself put up with that sloppy damn woman for all them years, and the only answer I could come up with was just that I hadn't knowed any better until right when I first laid eyes on Lillian.

"Good morning, sweetheart," Bonnie says, and she reached out for me, but I stepped back out of the way. I stuck me a long expensive cigar in my mouth, pulled out a match, and struck it on the tabletop. The flame flared up, and when it settled, I touched it to the end of my cigar and puffed till I had it going real good.

"Bonnie," I said, not wasting no time but getting right down to it, "we've had our good times, you and me, but it's all over with now."

"What?" she said, her jaw dropping down between her big tits and her bleary, red eyes popping open wide.

"I reckon you heard me right the first time," I said. "There ain't no sense in making a scene over this. It's just the way things is. These things happen, you know, and I hope there won't be no hard feelings between us. I think that we ought to keep on being good friends. After all, we're business partners still, and—"

"What the hell's got into you?" Bonnie said. "What are

you talking about?" And real fast she was up on her hands and knees on the bed, looking like some wild animal which was a-fixing to spring at me. "It's that woman, ain't it? That fancy hussy? Tell me the truth, you son of a bitch."

I give her a halfway smile then, and I said, "You wasn't calling me no son of a bitch last night." Well, I guess that wasn't the right thing to say just then. She roared out at me with all the power in her lungs, and that was considerable.

"Tell me," she hollered out, and she sounded downright savage.

When the walls had stopped shaking, I said, "Now, Bonnie, just calm down. I was hoping that we could stay friends. After all, we're in business here together."

"You already said that," she screamed at me.

"Now, take it easy, Bonnie," I said. "Hell, they can hear you clear downstairs."

"I don't give a damn who can hear me," she shrieked. "What the hell are you trying to pull on me?"

"I ain't trying to pull nothing," I said. "I just told you—"

"You tell me now what's going on," she said, and this time her voice was down low, but it was real menacing-like, it was kind of like a growl, and she was glaring hard at me. Her eyes wasn't wide no more. They had become mean-looking little slits, and her lips was pressed together so tight that I couldn't even see no lips at all, just a hard thin line underneath her nose.

"I'm fixing to get hitched up to Miss Lillian," I said. "That's all there is to it."

Well, I just thought that was all there was to it. Old Bonnie come up off that bed a-charging. She come at me with her claws all out and her fangs bared, just like an old wildcat. I reached up with both hands to protect myself, and I grabbed both of her wrists, but my God, she was strong for a woman. We staggered around like that for a bit, her trying to claw at my face and me trying to hold her back. I dropped my cigar on the floor, and right away Bonnie stepped on it with her bare foot, and she turned loose of me and went to hopping and screaming and holding her foot. I thought that looked like a pretty good time to make my exit, so I reached for my hat, which had also fell on the floor, but Bonnie pulled herself together real fast and kicked my ass so hard that I pitched on over on my face.

I scampered back up to my feet and turned to face her, to defend myself again, just as she grabbed up the water pitcher from off the table. I barely ducked out of the way when she throwed that thing at me, and it smashed against the wall just behind and beside me. I got a pretty good shower from it, all right. She was looking around for something else to toss at me, when I rushed her. I grabbed ahold of her and tossed her on her back onto the bed. I was meaning to hold her down and try to talk some calm into her, but she had managed to get one leg up, and she put her foot right in my paunch and shoved real hard, throwing me back. I crashed into the table that the water pitcher had come off of, and I just broke that little table all to pieces.

That hurt me some, but I've never been one to let a little hurt slow me down. "Goddamn you, Bonnie," I said, and I made ready to go at her again, but she had already came back up off of that bed, and she swung a roundhouse right that caught me right up on the side of my jaw. I seen little stars dancing around in front of my eyes from that. I staggered some and put both my hands up to my face, and she got both of her hands into my hair and commenced to shaking my head so hard I thought she'd yank out about a skein or two before she got done. Then she started into raising her knee up, trying to knee me in the balls. I had to get my hands down from my face and work at keeping that knee from doing some terrible damage to my manhood. All the time she was still shaking my head something fierce, and she was shrieking at me, "Son of a bitch. Son of a bitch."

Well, this had to come to a halt, and real soon. I seen that her elbows was wide apart, and both my hands was down low, holding her knee away from my vital parts, so I just come up real quick with a hard right-hand uppercut to her chin. Her knee dropped. Her hands relaxed and slipped loose from my hair, and she kind of leaned back away from me. I looked at her, and she was just standing there weaving, a kind of glazed-over look in her eyes. Then she fell over backward real stiff-like, and when she landed, her head bounced on the floor a time or two. I wondered for just a minute if I had maybe killed her, but when I seen them big tits heaving up and down from her breathing, I figured she was alive all right, and so I picked up my hat, dusted it off, and put it on my head.

I stepped up to the long mirror on the wall and straightened myself up as best I could. Then I took a deep breath and walked out of the room. I shut the door behind me and left her there. I knowed I'd have to face her again sooner or later, and I hoped that she would act with a little more restraint and dignity when that time come around. I walked down the hallway and then started down the stairs. There wasn't too many people down in the saloon part of the building, other than my own posse, but they was all looking at me, wondering, I guess, what all the racket from upstairs had been. I didn't give them no satisfaction, though. I just done my best to act like everything was normal, and I walked up to the bar and made old Aubrey pour me a glass of brown whiskey.

When I had took myself a good gulp, I turned around to look the room over. Dingle was setting there writing in his book, but I didn't give a damn about him. It was my posse I was concerned about. 'Course, old Gap Tooth was out there on them rocks watching the road, but everyone else should have been right there in Harvey's. I seen them all except two, and I guessed that they might be over at Maudie's having some grub or even upstairs with a couple of whores, early as it was, but I wanted to make sure.

"Where's them two drifters?" I said, not asking anyone in particular, just kind of asking the whole room. It was quiet for just a minute. Then Scratchy spoke up.

"You mean Snuff and Dusty?" he said.

"Them's the ones," I said, and I rubbed my jaw where Bonnie had just busted me one. It was some sore.

"They took off while you was . . ."

"While you was upstairs," said the Dutchman, helping old Scratchy out of a tough spot.

"What do you mean by that?" I said. "Where the hell'd they go?"

"They lit out, Barjack," the Dutchman said. "Saddled up their horses and left town."

I just stood there and burned for a few seconds. Then I took another slug of whiskey and thumped my glass down on the bar.

"All right, then," I said. "Let's go."

"Where to?" Scratchy asked.

"Get your horses," I ordered. I was feeling some military. "We're going after them deserting bastards."

I left Happy there in the Hooch House and Texas to watch the town, but I led the rest of them fellows out on the trail. With them two staying behind, Gap Tooth watching the road and two deserters out, that left me with a force of just only seven, and that counting me too. But I figured seven of us could handle them two chicken drifters. We got out to the rocks pretty damn quick, and I hollered up at Gap Tooth.

"Did them two goddamned drifters ride by here?" I said.

"Dusty and Snuff?" he asked.

"Who else?" I snapped back at him. I was feeling kind of cross. My jaw still hurt, and I had a headache from all that hair pulling. Being bounced up and down on a horse's back out in the hot sun wasn't helping matters none either.

"They rode by about ten minutes ago, I'd say," said Gap Tooth.

"Was they riding hard?" I asked.

"They sure was," he told me.

"Come on," I said to my posse. "Let's get them."

I led the boys on out the road, but I kept us going along at an easy pace. I figured them drifters would wear out their mounts pretty soon, and then we'd come up on them right casual. I figured right. We found them not far from the very place where I had took Lillian, watering their horses and catching their breath. I spread the posse out till it was seven of us riding abreast, and we all got guns in our hands and started in riding toward them, real slow-like.

"You boys throw down your guns," I called out to them. "We're taking you in."

"What for?" Dusty yelled back at me.

"You ain't lived up to our deal," I said.

"We ain't going back," said Snuff.

"One way or the other," I said, "you are."

Then both of them drifters went for the six-guns at their sides, and all seven of us commenced to shooting at once. We was shooting six-guns too, and the range was still considerable for a handgun, so our shots was hitting all round them, kicking up dust and making a hell of a racket. I don't think Dusty or Snuff either one ever got off a single shot. They just throwed their arms up around their heads like they was trying to protect themselves from a hailstorm or something. And they was kind of dancing around, hopping on one foot and then the other. Finally I put a stop to it.

"Hold your fire," I called out, and there was one or two shots after that, but then everyone quit. I expect that all our six-shooters was done shot out, but I didn't say nothing about that, and it probably never occurred to Dusty and Snuff neither. "Throw down your shooters," I told them, and they did. I had the Dutchman dismount and gather up their weapons while Scratchy tied the fugitives' hands behind their backs. Then I told Chicago to gather up their horses by the reins and lead them along with us back to town.

"Hey," Snuff said, slowly figuring things out, "what about us?"

"Get to walking," I said. I made them two walk along in front of us all the way back to the Asininity jailhouse, and then I locked them back up in the same cell where they had been before. They was real wore out, I can tell you. They started in to begging me to let their hands loose and to give them a drink of water, but I just ignored them for a while. "You two assholes should've thought at least twice before you double-crossed me," I said. I hoped that this would be a lesson to the rest of my posse that once they had signed on with me to do a job, they had best stick to it till the whole damned job was over and done.

I thought about changing my clothes, but then I told myself to hell with it. I wanted some whiskey real bad, so I just walked back to the Hooch House just the way I was, and I was a kind of a mess. I had on my best suit, sure enough, but then I had tangled with old Bonnie, got doused good with water, and then had rode out on that dusty old road. I decided that I didn't give a damn, though. I wanted to get drunk. In the Hooch House, I told Happy and Aubrey both to make sure that my posse stayed sober,'cause I meant to get real stinky-face drunk. They assured me that they'd see to it. I thought for just a minute about Lillian and how she deserved more from me than that, but then I promised myself that I'd give up that kind of drinking starting first thing in the morning. Then I considered the possibility that old Bonnie would come to and come downstairs and take advantage of my condition to do me serious harm, and I walked over to Happy a-setting on his perch.

"Happy," I said in a kind of a low voice, "I done told you my intentions. Now, listen good to this." He took on a real serious look and nodded his head, leaning down toward me so he could hear me real good. "Old Bonnie's for sure pissed off at me," I continued on. "If you see her come at me, and I ain't in no condition to defend myself, just shoot her dead right then and there."

"Shoot a woman?" Happy said, incredulous-like.

"You heard me right," I said. "Better her than me, and by God, Happy, I mean it. She threatened my life, so you'd be preventing a murder."

Then I went back to the bar and set about with hard determination to accomplish my previous stated purpose.

Chapter Nine

Well, I commenced with a tumbler full of my favorite brown whiskey, and I don't know how much of that hooch I drunk, but before long I had done accomplished my mission. I was drunk for sure. I was staggering drunk. I couldn't hardly make my words come out the way I meant them to. I was seeing double most of the time, and the whole damned room seemed to be spinning all around, and I felt like that if I wasn't real careful, whenever the floor tilted off real steep to one side, I would go sliding off to somewhere, so I was hanging on to chairs or a table or the front edge of the bar—whatever I could keep a tight hold of to anchor myself with. It must have been pretty late in the afternoon by then, and I know that I was about ready to pass out, when I seen through the fuzziness of what was left of my vision old Bonnie a-flouncing her way down the stairs. Her big tits was really bouncing. I could see that even fuzzy. I managed to turn my head enough to give a look at Happy over there on his perch, and I seen him tense up, and I knowed that he seen her too and was thinking about what he might have to do.

I thought right then that there was fixing to be some blood let in the Hooch House that night, and I was hoping that it wouldn't be mine. But then, I wasn't too worried. For one thing, I was too drunk to be able to think straight enough to worry much. But the main thing was that I knowed that old Happy had his orders, and I knowed that he was watching Bonnie's every move. I was trying to keep one eye on Bonnie and one eye on Happy, but then that's a pretty good trick even when you're sober. So I moved my head kind of slow from one to the other. Even that slow movement was kind of dangerous to my equilibrium, considering the state I was in. I did see Bonnie walk on over to the bar, though, and I kind of thought that I could tell that she had ordered something. That seemed like a good sign to me. Likely she just needed a stiff drink after what she had gone through with me earlier in the day.

I relaxed a little then, and my head rolled back over toward old Happy, and then I seen him tense up even more and hop down off his perch and come a-headed toward me, but he wasn't looking at me. He seemed to be looking just past me. I turned my head as fast as I could, which wasn't very fast, but it sure made the room spin faster when I did it, and then I seen through a kind of a blur old Bonnie, and she was just almost right on me. She had a nearly full whiskey bottle in her right hand, and she already had it up high, ready to swing. The last thing I seen was that bottle coming at me and a fuzzy image of old Dingle a-watching from back behind, and then that bottle crashed hard against the side of my head and shattered. It didn't hurt me none, though. I never felt a thing. I was out cold too damn fast for it to hurt.

August 11

I come to on the cot in the cell right next door to the one the two drifters was in. I come to real slow, too. I didn't know what time it was or what day it was. I was groggy, and my head hurt like hell. I started to set up, but it was way too much work, and it just hurt me worse, so I eased myself on back down with a low groan. I heard a voice come at me from the next-door cell, but I couldn't tell which drifter it was doing the talking. "Serves you right, you son of a bitch," it said. I reckoned that it probably did, but I didn't say nothing about it one way or the other. I just lay there a-moaning low. Then I heard footsteps, and they sure did sound loud. I eased my eyes open and took a careful look, and it was old Texas Jack Dooly. He brought a chair on into the cell and put it there beside the cot and set down.

"Barjack," he said, and he kept his voice low. He knowed better than to talk to me too loud, the state that I was in. I must have rolled my head a little toward him and squinted. "Barjack, you all right?"

"Hell, no," I said. "Goddamn. I ain't never been this drunk before. I never did pass out that hard in my whole damned life."

"Hell, boss," he said. "You didn't pass out. You was knocked out."

Slowly it come back to me, the blurry image of Bonnie swinging that whiskey bottle, and I moaned again and put a hand up to my head. I felt crusted-up blood in my hair and down the side of my face. I glanced down at my shirt-front and seen it all bloodstained too.

"Oh, yeah," I said. "I kind of recollect now. How the hell did I get over here?"

"Chicago and Shorty Joe hauled you over," Texas said. "They said that just as soon as you hit the floor, Bonnie yelled out for someone to get you the hell out of there before she decided to finish you off. So they done it."

I let that soak in for a minute, and then I was recalling the orders I had give to Happy and the fact that I had seen him headed my way just before the lights went out.

"What about Happy?" I said, and it still hurt to talk, so I groaned again.

"Well, from what I heard," Texas said, "he was standing there a-looking at Bonnie, and she still had the neck of that broke bottle in her hand. She asked him what the hell he wanted, and then he told her that you had give him orders to shoot her dead if she was to come for you. She stared at him real hard, and I guess he just turned away from her. He told Chicago, who was just right there at the next table, he told him to tell you, whenever you was to wake up, that he had quit. He said he didn't hire on with you to shoot no women."

"Happy's quit?" I said. I couldn't hardly believe that. Why, old Happy'd been with me for a long time, and I could tell him just anything to do and he'd do it. I didn't know what to think about that. I couldn't hardly imagine what it would look like in the Hooch House without old Happy a-setting there on his perch. "He can't do that," I said, and I tried again to set up, but I couldn't make it. Texas put his hands on my shoulders like he was trying to settle me back down, but there wasn't no need for it. I went back down of my own.

"He's done left town, Barjack," he said.

"Well, go after him," I said. "Bring him back here."

"You going to walk him back to town and lock him in here with us?" said Snuff, calling out from the next-door cell. I had forgot all about them two.

"Tell them to shut up," I said to Texas. "Or else take them out and hang them."

"He's right, Barjack," Texas said. "We can't go after Happy and bring him back if he don't want to come back. He just had a job, and he quit it. That's all. Hell, a man can quit a job if he's a mind to. Them two was in jail when you made your deal with them. That's different. They was like—what do you call it? They was kind of like on . . . probation."

"We was railroaded," Dusty yelled.

"Shut up," said Texas. "You ever want to get them hands of your untied?"

"We'll get us a lawyer," Dusty said, "and we'll sue your ass for false arrest by a corrupt lawman and then cruel treatment of prisoners while incarcerated in jail. That's what we'll do."

Texas stood up and made like he was leaving the cell.

"Hell, Marshal," he said, "I guess I will go on and hang them like you said."

"Now, Deputy," said Snuff, "Dusty ain't going to say no more, and he didn't mean that about getting a lawyer."

"Well, all right, then," Texas said, "but keep your yaps shut."

Well, I was slowly coming back to life, and then I did set up, but it sure did hurt like hell's fire. My old head was throbbing something fierce. So Bonnie had coldcocked me, and then instead of shooting the bitch dead like he was supposed to have did, old Happy had up and quit on me and even rode out of town. I already had two deserters locked back up in jail, and now with Happy gone, my twelve-man posse was suddenly down to nine. As bad as I was feeling, I still thought that nine ought to be enough to get the job done.

"Texas, what time of day has it got to be?" I asked.

"It's about ten," Texas said.

I could see light coming in through the front windows of the office, and I wrinkled my face up squinting at it. "It ain't dark out," I said.

"It's ten in the morning," said Texas. "Hell, Barjack, you was out cold all night along."

"Well, goddamn," I said, and I looked over at the two drifters with their hands tied behind their backs. I didn't feel sorry for them. Hell, I'd just as soon have took them out somewhere and strung them up like I had suggested, but I didn't really see no sense in torturing them either. "Untie them two," I said, "and give them some water. Then see if you can't get Maudie to send them over some of that greasy hash of hers."

"Okay," Texas said. He give them a look like he didn't really think they was worth the trouble, and then he started to leave the cell. He looked back at me, setting there on the edge of that cot and holding my head in both hands. "You okay?" he asked me.

"Yeah," I said. "I'm okay. Go on ahead."

While Texas went about doing as I had told him to do, I started out testing my legs. I stood up real slow, waited a bit, then started to walk. I walked on down the short hallway to the room I had in back where I could sleep and where I kept some clothes and stuff. There was a little table with a water pitcher and a bowl on it. A mirror was on the wall just behind it, and a towel was hanging there on a peg. I sloshed some water in the bowl and dipped my hands down in it, leaning over, but before I got my face down in the water, I seen it in the mirror. God almighty, I was a hell of a mess. I stared at myself for a while, wondering just what could have got into Bonnie Boodle to mess me up like that after all we had been through together over the years and all we had once meant to each other. I finally figured that's all you can expect from a goddamned whore.

It was painful, but I managed to wash my face up, and then I got out of my ruined suit and into some clean clothes. I thought about going after Happy the way I done them drifters, but then I decided that Texas had probably been right about that. I didn't really have no legal reason to go after him. Besides, he had a pretty damn good head start on me, and besides that, it didn't really make me mad that Happy had ran out on me. It made me kind of sad. I made up my mind, though, that if I ever seen him again, I was going to knock his goddamned block off, and then if he wanted to know why, I wouldn't tell him. I wouldn't say nothing. Just leave him laying there wondering and walk away.

I wanted to see Lillian real bad, but I kind of hated to let her see me the way I was looking, and I needed a bath to get all the whiskey stink off of me. The only place I had ever had a bath had been up in Bonnie's room, and I sure as hell wasn't going to get naked anywhere she might be able to get ahold of me. By the time I had cleaned up my face a little and come out of the back room, Texas was back and the drifters was chowing down. They was so hungry and so busy eating, they didn't even cuss me none when I walked by.

"Texas," I said, "run down and see old Porkbarrel for me. Tell him I want me a bathtub rigged up and stuck in that back room there. Tell him I want it right away, too."

92

"A bathtub?" said Texas.

"That's what I said. Go on and tell him now," I snapped back, and Texas shoved his hat down on his head and took off. I looked over at them drifters scarfing down that greasy hash from Maudie's, and for just a minute I thought about turning them loose, but then I recalled how much they had pissed me off by running out on me the way they done, and I decided to let them stew in there for a while longer. I walked over to old Peester's office to find out what he might know about the five empty buildings what used to be saloons. He had the control of them all right, just like I figured he would.

I decided that the likeliest place for my new restaurant and hotel would be the building that I had thought of before, the biggest one, the one that had once been the old Watering Hole, and I told Peester to fix up the paperwork so I could go ahead and buy it. He said that he would, and I left again. Then I got to thinking about them Bensons again, and then I remembered that I had left poor old Gap Tooth out there on them rocks for a hell of a long time. I hustled back to the Hooch House, telling myself that I wouldn't drink no whiskey and take no chance on getting drunk again with Bonnie around anywhere nearby. I walked in and there was the most of my posse still just a-setting in there, and that damned sissy Dingle was talking to two of them and still writing things down in his pad. That annoyed me some, but I didn't have time to worry over it. I didn't see Bonnie though, and I was glad of that.

"Say," I said, "why hasn't anyone gone out there to relieve old Gap Tooth?"

"You never told no one to go," said the Dutchman.

"Well, I'm telling you now," I said. "Get your ass on out there. I reckon he's pretty tired and hungry by now, so hurry on up."

The Dutchman left, and then I did too. I thought that if I stayed in there any longer, I might just be tempted to kick Dingle's little sissy ass. And I didn't want to deal with Bonnie no more. At least not just then. I figured that if she was to come down, I might just go on ahead and kill her my own self. She had cracked my head and caused me to lose old Happy, and I couldn't hardly forgive her for neither one of them things. I strolled on out of there, stopped by the general store and bought myself a new suit of clothes, and then I went on back down to the office. Texas was back, and there was a hell of a racket coming from the back room, where I figured old Porkbarrel was banging away at my new bathtub. I went back there to take a look.

"How long's this going to take you?" I asked him.

"I ought to be done in another hour," Porkbarrel said. "It was mostly done anyhow. An old water trough, it was."

"It'll do," I said, "long as it holds water."

"It won't leak," Porkbarrel said. "I g'arantee that."

I put my new clothes on the cot in there and walked back out into the office. Texas was setting in my chair with his feet up on my desk. I took the big key ring off the peg on the wall and tossed it on the desk in front of him.

"Go on ahead and open up that cell door," I said.

He dropped his feet to the floor and looked toward the cell with the drifters in it. "That one there?" he said.

"Ain't no other cell door locked, is there?" I said. "Sometimes I think I ought to get myself a keyhole saw and a bucket of brains and fix you up to where you're like a normal human being. Go on and unlock it."

He stood up, picked up the keys, and went to do what I said. Soon as he was out of the way, I took over my chair. I opened up a desk drawer and took out the drifters' gunbelts. I emptied the guns of their bullets and reholstered them. Glancing over, I could see that them two was hesitating, not knowing what I was up to. Maybe they was afraid that I was going to hang them after all. "Come on out of there, you assholes," I said. "I don't want the town to have to feed you no more."

They walked out, kind of slow and cautious, and stepped over to the front of my desk. I tossed their rigs toward them. "Take them," I said. "Go on and get your horses and ride on out of town. Don't waste no time about it, neither. I don't never want to see neither one of you bastards around here again."

They grabbed up their rigs and headed for the door. Just as they was going out, old Snuff looked back over his shoulder. "You won't," he said. And I never did. Not in Asininity.

Chapter Ten

I made old Texas Jack help me out, and we boiled up several pots of water on the old potbellied stove there in the office. It heated up the office somewhat too, it being a hot August day, but we opened up the door and all the windows, and pretty soon I had me a tub full of hot water in the back room. I was damn near naked, though, before I realized that I didn't have no soap in the place, so I sent Texas after some. When he come back with it, he let me know for certain that he was plumb embarrassed about being sent to buy soap. He said there was some smart-assed cowboys in there at the store at the time that seen him, and he thought that they was laughing at him behind his back. If he could have been for sure about it, he'd have whipped them real good, he said. He told me then that if I ever done him that way again, he'd up and quit me for sure and ride out after old Happy. I promised him that it wouldn't never happen again, and then I had me a long hot soak and a good wash. I was still setting there in that soapy water whenever I heard someone crashing through the front door. In a minute Texas come in on me with the Dutchman right behind him.

"Someone's killed poor old Gap Tooth," the Dutchman said.

I guess I must have looked like my eyes was about to pop out. "Who done it?" I said. 'Course, I thought right away about the damned Bensons. It was a mite early yet for them to be in town, if they was sticking to their word that they sent me in that telegram, but I didn't trust them none. Besides, who else would it be killing my deputy? The Dutchman shrugged.

"I don't know," he said. "I just found him out there. He'd been blasted in the back with a shotgun, looked like. Looked to me like he'd been there like that for a while, too. Flies was swarming all over him. I loaded him up on his horse and brought him on into town."

"Well, who the hell's out watching the road, then?" I said, and I was so excited that I stood right up right there in front of them, and me stark staring naked and dripping water and soap suds.

"No one's out there right now," the Dutchman said. "Hell, I had to bring Gap Tooth in, didn't I?"

"Well, get your ass back out there," I said. "Hurry it up."

"Not by myself, I ain't," he said. "I don't want no one to come out there and find me the same way I found old Gap Tooth. All blasted away like that. No, sir."

"Go over to the Hooch House, then, and tell the rest of the boys to gather up over here," I said. "Then take Chicago with you on back out to the rocks. Go on, now. Get."

The Dutchman took right off then, and I grabbed myself a towel. By the time the boys had gathered in my office, I was dried off and dressed again, but not in my new suit of clothes. I had bought them to go calling on Lillian, and now I was going to have to put that off for a while. We all mounted up and rode out to the rocks to look things over. I think I mentioned to you before that Texas wasn't none too bright, but one thing about that boy for sure, he could read sign. He was a damn good tracker—one of the best I ever seen. I heard someone say once that that old boy could track a damned cockroach across a wood floor. After we had poked around for some time, old Texas, who had been down on all fours a-sniffing the ground or something, straightened himself up and stretched his back.

"They was just one man," he said. "I'd say he slipped up behind Gap Tooth. He come in from across the flats there. Sneaked up on him and blowed him away. Just like that. Likely poor old Gap Tooth never seen him and never knowed what hit him."

"Just one man, eh?" I said. "I wonder where the other three are at."

"I don't think it was the Bensons," Texas said. "I can't figure them to split up like that, knowing that you're going to be ready for them here. And I can't see any one of them swinging way around off the road like that to come up behind old Gap Tooth the way this one done. I think this fella was riding a mule, too."

"How can you tell that?" I asked him.

"I can tell," he said.

Well, I sure as hell hated to split up my dwindled-down posse, but I couldn't hardly let poor old Gap Tooth's killer just run loose, neither. Besides, Texas might have been wrong about who done it. It might have been a Benson. But neither could I leave Asininity unprotected. The Bensons was still coming, and I didn't know just when they would ride on in. And like I said, I wasn't total convinced that Texas was right about who it was had killed old Gap Tooth. I thought that maybe the Bensons was already somewhere nearby. It made my skin crawl thinking about it. I told Texas to take Shorty Joe and Ten-Gallon along with him and track down the killer, and I left Chicago and the Dutchman there at the rocks. Then I rode on back into town with the other two. I sure was feeling vulnerable, I can tell you, with my strength all scattered like that. It had never occurred to me that anyone would sneak into town from across open country.

The three of us rode back into town, and I had Scratchy stop by the Hooch House and pick up a bottle of whiskey to bring on over to the office. I still wasn't feeling like spending no time over there with Bonnie still around and still murderous. I told the boys to help themselves to a drink and that I'd be right back to join them shortly. Then I went by to see old Peester. I told him that I wanted him to go see Bonnie and tell her that I wanted to buy out her interest in the Hooch House and then I wanted her to get her round ass out of town. I told him to tell her that if she didn't agree to that, that I'd have to arrest her for assaulting an officer of the law and hold her in jail till the judge come around sometime next month. He wasn't none too hot on the idea, but after reminding me that he would send me a bill for all his services, he did finally promise to take care of that little chore for me.

I left the skinflint bastard there in his office, and then I rode horseback on over to my new house to see Lillian for just long enough to let her know that I hadn't forgot her but that things had been hopping for me somewhat that day. She told me in her sweet voice that she understood, and she made over my busted head, which I never told her just how I got it. I did tell her that I had gone ahead and actual made the deal for the building for our hotel and restaurant, and I did say "our," and that just tickled her for sure. It made me feel good too. I sure did hate to leave her there, but I figured I had ought to be back with the boys waiting and watching for the Bensons and looking for Texas and the others to get back and report on their luck.

I did ask her before I left if she had everything she needed, and she told me that she had ventured out all by her lonesome and had a couple of meals that day over at Maudie's. I felt kind of bad about that, but there wasn't no place else, and I hadn't exactly been much help to her that day. I promised to come out the next morning and bring a load of groceries and spend some time with her, and then I tore myself away and went on back to the office, where I poured me a big glass of whiskey and set myself down behind my desk. Remuda and Scratchy had already poured themselves some of the good stuff and was happily sipping at it when I come in.

"Reckon when the other boys'll be back," Scratchy said.

"No telling," said Remuda. "The Dutchman told us he thought Gap Tooth had been laying dead there for quite a spell. Whoever done the killing likely has a good start on them."

"What we have to do," I said, "is just keep our mind on our own business. The Bensons could come riding in at just any time. There's four of them, and right now until Texas and them gets back, there's only three of us. I don't like them odds much."

"Well, what should we do?" Scratchy asked.

I downed my whiskey and set down the glass. Then I stood up and hitched at my britches. "Drink up," I said. "We'll get us up on top of some of the buildings and watch the streets from there. If I see a Benson, I'll start shooting. Then you two do the same. Take a rifle with you."

We was still laying on the rooftops when Texas and them rode back in. The sun was real low in the sky by that time. I seen right away that there was a woman riding behind Texas's saddle, and Shorty Joe was leading a mule all right, and there was a carcass throwed across it. I wondered again how old Texas had knowed them was mule tracks, and then I wondered about that cockroach story too. 'Course, I also wondered who the damn woman was and where she had came from. I waved at Scratchy, who was on a roof across the street and hollered. Pretty soon all six of us met down in the street in front of my office. Texas helped the woman get off from behind him, and I seen that it was Tootie, old Gap Tooth's runaway wife, and then Texas swung down out of his saddle and sauntered over to where the head of the carcass was dangling down at the side of that mule. He grabbed it by the hair and lifted it up to show me the face. By God, he was right again. It wasn't no Benson at all. That was for damn sure.

"Well, I'll be goddamned," I said. "Fin Brackett."

"What the hell would Fin want to kill Gap Tooth for?" asked Remuda.

"Fin run off with Gap Tooth's wife," Texas said.

"So?" said Remuda, giving a casual shrug. "What'd he want to kill Gap Tooth for?"

Texas scratched the top of his head and wrinkled his face up some. "I don't know," he said. "But he done it. That much is for sure."

"Well," I said, "I reckon the best we can say is that there was bad blood betwixt them. They're both dead now. Unless we can get Miz Harman here to tell us something about it."

"You can try if you want to, Marshal," Texas said, "but she ain't been willing to say more than go to hell to me. We found her and Fin back at the Harman house, and my guess is that the two of them was in on it together."

"Yeah?" I said, giving old Tootie a hard look. She just glared back at me, and I figured that old Texas had been right about her. Likely her and old Fin had decided to do away with poor old Gap Tooth before Gap Tooth took a notion to go after them. "You better come along with me, Tootie," I said.

"I'll get someone to take care of the stiff," said Texas. He took the mule's reins away from Shorty Joe and started across the street. I sent Scratchy and Remuda out to the rocks to relieve the other two cowboys, and I went back inside the office with Tootie Harman and locked her up in a cell. Directly old Peester come in to see me. He seen Tootie right away.

"What's she doing in there?" he said.

"I'm holding her for questioning on suspicion of the murder of Gap Tooth Harman," I said. "She's old Gap Tooth's wife—well, now his widow. She run off with Fin Brackett, and Fin killed Gap Tooth. We suspect her of being in on the deed."

"Just what do you plan to do with her?" Peester said.

"Actual," I said, "the killing took place outside of town, so I reckon I'll have to deliver her over to old Dick Custer first chance I get and leave him to worry on it."

"Well, I talked to Bonnie," Peester said, but he seemed just a bit reluctant to leave off on the subject of the widow Harman.

"Well, then?" said I. "What the hell did she say? Is she going to leave town?"

"She said she'll buy you out," Peester said, "but she's damned if she'll let you run her out of business and out of town. And furthermore, she said, if you want to arrest her, go right on ahead. She said she'd just love to get you in a court of law and tell the whole world everything she knows on you."

"Goddamn her," I said.

"What do you plan to do now?" Peester asked me, and he was looking kind of stern, the way only a lawyer or a preacher or a teacher can look at you. I was burning up over what he had just told me, so I didn't answer him right away. I didn't know the answer to his question anyhow. I was trying to figure out in my head just what old Bonnie's threat meant. I wasn't sure if she could tell anything that would cause me problems or not. Sure as hell, I'd done something sometime or other that was at least in the gray areas of the law, but I didn't know if she knowed anything for certain sure that could prove that I had done something that was actual illegal. I figured that I had better mull this over for a spell.

The problem was that I didn't think that I really had enough cash to buy old Bonnie out, not and go ahead and redo my new properties the way I wanted to do them. And if I was to turn loose of my interest in the Hooch House, why, I'd lose the biggest portion of my income. My marshaling pay wasn't all that much. 'Course, a lot might just depend on how much she'd be willing to pay for my controlling share. And there was a serious question in my mind as to whether a respectable hotel and restaurant would even do very well in Asininity anyhow. I had figured that the Hooch House would kind of, you know, carry along the other businesses on its back. It wasn't a pleasant thought, but I considered that I just might have to go on indefinite with old Bonnie as my business partner. At least for a spell. That is, until I could think up some permanent solution to the goddamned problem.

"All right," I said, "ask her how much she's willing to pay me for my interest," I said to Peester, not really caring much,'cause I sure didn't want to sell out to her, but it was something to say to him to answer his question and to get him the hell out of there.

"I'll ask her," he said. Then he paused a couple of seconds before changing the subject. "Just what is it that she has got on you anyway?" he asked me.

"What do you mean?" I said. 'Course, I knowed exactly what he meant, but I let on I didn't have no idea.

"If you were to get her in court," he said, "what could she tell on you?"

"Nothing," I said. "What could she? She's bluffing, that's all."

"Then why are you not following through with your threat to arrest her?" the sly old lawyer said.

"Aw," I said, "that was just something I said to try to get her to agree to sell out to me. I never would have really did that to her. Why, me and old Bonnie has meant a lot to each other over the years. Hell, you ought to know that."

Peester looked like he didn't really buy that, but there wasn't much he could say about it, so he excused himself and headed on out, and I was glad to be rid of him. I always have thought that a lawyer is a worse crook than a bank robber. The only problem is that it ain't legal to shoot them down in the street the way you would other outlaws. Even so, I needed the son of a bitch's services from time to time. Texas Jack come back in just about that time.

Well, I finished the whiskey that was in my glass, and I went back to the back room and checked myself over in the mirror there. I spiffed myself up just a little, and then I left Texas in charge of things and walked over to my new house to see Lillian. She hadn't ate her supper yet, so I walked her over to Maudie's and we had us a bite to eat. I told her most of the news from that day, about old Gap Tooth getting himself killed, and my deputies tracking down and killing the killer. I told her again that I had bought the old Watering Hole to redo into our hotel and restaurant, and she got all excited again about that. I had to promise her that we'd go down and take a look at it first thing in the morning. The truth is that I'd have been pretty excited about it myself if it hadn't been for thinking about the Bensons and Bonnie Boodle.

Chapter Eleven

August 12

I picked up Lillian about nine that morning, and we had us a breakfast at Maudie's. Then we went on over to the former Watering Hole, and I unlocked the front door and we went inside to look it over. It was dusty and some run-down, having just set empty like that for so long, but Lillian thought it was just marvelous. She figured out where the restaurant would go there in that big room that had been a saloon, and she planned out where the desk for the hotel would be. We even went upstairs and looked at the little bitty whore rooms, and she said we could knock out some walls and make some real nice hotel rooms out of them. Neither one of us ever said a word about why them rooms was so little and why they didn't have no closets for clothes or nothing like that. We spent a good part of the morning looking that building over and making plans for it, and then Lillian really took me by surprise.

"Barjack," she said, and she stepped up real close to me and put her hands on my shoulders and smiled up into my face, "why do we have to wait? Let's get married right away. I know you've got serious business taking up your time just now, but I've committed myself to you. And while you're getting all that unpleasantness taken care of, I could get started on this building. What do you say, darling?"

Well, she had never called me that before, and the sound of it just melted my old hard heart. The truth is that I had suggested waiting in the first place more for her sake than for mine. I hadn't thought that it would be fair to marry up with her and then get myself killed by either the Bensons or by old Bonnie. But by God, if she was willing to go on ahead with it, knowing the dangers involved and all, why, then why the hell not? Then, if it should come about that I was to get myself killed, why, I'd have had myself a heavenly honeymoon night first. I was almost thinking that might even be worth it.

So we went over to see old Peester, and then I got myself a big surprise. There wasn't no way to get a license to marry up or to find anyone authorized to marry us up there in Asininity. Peester said that we'd have to go over to the county seat for that. Then he said that what we could do was we could just go on ahead and move in together and live like man and wife and after some time had gone by we'd be just as married as if we'd done it the other way. He called it common law or something like that. But I had too much respect for Lillian to do that. There wouldn't be nothing common for her if I could help it. So I decided that we'd make the thirty-mile ride on over to the county seat, and me and Lillian together decided that we'd do it first thing the next morning.

Well, I sure had me some tall thinking to do. Part of it had to do with old Bonnie, goddamn her hide. I didn't figure that she'd take the news any too good, and I was still trying to figure out a way to get her out of town and keep the Hooch House for myself. I considered killing her off, but I didn't really want to do that, not unless I had to. Another part of it was my now shaky finances. As soon as we was all hitched up proper, Lillian would start in to spending my money on the old Watering Hole, and I was afraid that I might run some short. I didn't want to tell her that, though. And then there was the big one. There was the thirty-mile ride down that lonesome road from Asininity on over to the county seat, and it was the same goddamned road that I figured the Bensons would be traveling on when they was headed into town to do my ass in real final-like. I'd have to think on that one awhile.

Well, we picked up a mess of groceries, and then I took Lillian on over to the house, where we had us some lunch. We give each other real proper kind of pecks on the cheek, and I headed back to my office. I had some things to work out, for sure. I knowed that it wouldn't look right for me to just ride out of town for a couple or three days and not leave anyone to protect the town. So I couldn't take my whole damn posse with me. I'd have to leave Texas in charge there in Asininity. There just didn't seem to be no way around that one. But I figured he could handle things in town all by his own self. There wasn't likely to be no real trouble. If the real trouble was coming in that day, the rest of us would be the ones to meet it out there on the road. There would be me, Shorty Joe, Ten-Gallon, Chicago, Remuda, Scratchy, and the Dutchman. We ought to be able to handle four Bensons, I figured.

Anyhow, I found Texas in the office with his feet on my desk, and I made him get up and let me have my own chair. He had a pot of coffee on, but I wanted something stronger, so I hauled the bottle out of my desk drawer and poured myself a tumbler of good brown whiskey. Then I commenced to telling Texas my plans for the next day. He scratched his head the way he does, and then he said, "So you're really fixing to get hitched up proper."

"Yeah," I said. "What about it?" I felt kind of like he had just accused me of planning to do something terrible, like kick a little kid or a dog or something. "You trying to make something of it?"

"No," he said. "Hell no. Not me. She's a right smart lady, I reckon. I was just thinking about Bonnie, that's all."

"Bonnie ain't got nothing to do with this," I said.

"I reckon not," said Texas, "but I wonder if she'll agree with us on that matter."

Well, I knowed that old Texas was right about that. I knowed that I hadn't heard the last from old Bonnie either, and she was going to cause me some kind of real trouble sooner or later. Right then I thought again about how I might do her in and not get caught at it, but I just couldn't come up with no idea. I was for sure going to have to do something about it, though. I knowed that much. I didn't answer him, though. I just set there a-thinking.

"Barjack," Texas said.

"Yeah?" I muttered.

"It's a long day's ride over to the county seat," he said.

"Hell, I know that," I said.

"Another day getting back. If you got any business to take care of," he went on, "you might be gone for three days."

"So?" I said.

"In three days it'll be the fifteenth," he said. "Them Bensons'll be here."

I have to admit that I hadn't been counting all that good. That thought startled me some. I couldn't hardly change my plans at that point, though. I couldn't bring myself to tell Lillian that the Bensons had scared me off of our wedding, and so we'd have to do it later. I considered staying in Asininity and sending someone to the county seat to fetch me back a preacher, but that didn't set right with me. I knowed it wouldn't set good with Lillian, either. Then it come to me.

"Texas," I said. "There's a change in plans."

"What?" he said.

"You're going with us in the morning," I said.

"To the county seat?" he said. I groaned a little at how thick his skull could be at times.

"Where else?" I said. "That's where the hell we're going, ain't it?"

"Well, what about Asininity?" he said. "You going to leave it without no law with the Bensons a-coming in?"

"If them Bensons get here and don't find me in town,"

I said, "they ain't going to do a damn thing. They ain't going to want to take no chance on getting into trouble and getting throwed back in jail without they've killed me first."

Texas scratched his head. "You might be right about that," he said.

"And besides, if you and me and the whole posse is either out on the road or, better yet, over at the county seat with the sheriff and all his deputies when the Bensons comes along, we'll meet them away from Asininity and the odds'll be a damn site better, don't you think?" I said.

"Yeah," he said, as if he'd sudden seen a flash of light. "I think you got something there, Marshal."

"If we're headed that way," I said, "and they're headed this way, they can't get here anyhow without they run into us."

"Yeah," Texas said.

So it was settled, and then I actual got to hoping that we would be right there in the county seat when them four come riding through on their way into Asininity. I told myself that the first thing I'd do when I got over there was to drop in on the sheriff, old Dick Custer, and let him know just what the hell was up. Then he could alert all his deputies, and we could all lay in wait together for them Bensons. Hell, there wouldn't be nothing to it. We'd wipe their ass out with no trouble at all, and I'd get myself hitched up proper with Lillian, and then we'd all head back home. Me and my new wife would settle in there at my new house, and we'd get right to work on the restaurant and hotel. The only fly in the beer was that I'd still have old Bonnie to deal with, but I decided not to worry about her for the time being. I'd take care of first things first.

"Texas," I said, "round up the boys and tell them to all get ready for a ride tomorrow. Tell them to meet me at my new house at first light. And tell old Porkbarrel to have me a buggy ready to go too. His best one, with that old gray mare of his hitched up to it. Oh, yeah. And in the morning, you bring along the prisoner."

"The prisoner?" he said.

"You heard me right," I said. "You bring along old Tootie there, and we'll hand her over to the county sheriff. Now, get going, will you?"

Texas headed out to do what all I had told him to do, and I set there alone at my desk sipping my whiskey. Things was looking up, I thought. But I still felt like I needed to do some more scheming to turn this situation even more to my advantage. It was just possible, I told myself, that old Dick Custer would take the same kind of small-minded attitude as had Peester the first time I had approached him. He might just up and say that there was nothing we could do to the Bensons, not till they had actual up and killed me. He never had near as liberal-thinking a mind as what I had.

Then it come on me that I could try to somehow tie old Gap Tooth's killing to the Bensons. I could say that we had found old Gap Tooth killed while he was a-watching for them. That had ought to be near enough. But then one of my blabbermouth deputies might let out that we had killed old Fin Brackett for the doing of that deed, and of course, we would have Tootie Harman along as a suspect. I thought that if I was lucky, though, she'd still be keeping her mouth shut. Well, okay, so maybe I could sort of imply that old Fin and maybe even Tootie along with him had been working with the Bensons, sort of scouting things out for them. And then, of course, old Gap Tooth had been killed outside of Asininity. By rights that put the whole entire crime under the county jurisdiction and made it old Dick Custer's business whether he wanted it or not. I wondered if he'd be pissed off that I had even sent my posse out after Fin, but I didn't think that he would mind that too much. Goddamn, I hoped that I could convince him that the Bensons was behind it all.

Well, it come to me at last that I would damn sure try to do it that way. Unless we was to run up against them Bensons while we was on the road to the county seat, and thereby kill them all off early, I would tell Custer that the Bensons was coming to kill me and that they had snookered Fin and Tootie into working for them. Old Fin had already gone and killed one of my deputies. I thought then that I might as well also say that he had somehow managed to run off two more. I was thinking of them two drifters, Dusty and Snuff. I felt good about all my thinking, and I decided that I'd go on over to my new house and have a good supper with my lovely fiancée.

Chapter Twelve

August 13

We started out in the morning with the sun, headed toward the county seat. I was driving old Porkbarrel's best buggy again, pulled by his old gray mare, and my sweetest of sweets was setting right there beside me looking and smelling like the most wonderful thing that God ever put down here on this earth. I was dressed in my best, and I had even took me a bath just that morning, too. I reckon I was driving along with my head held up right high and snooty-like. We was toting along with us a great big picnic basket chock-full of all kinds of good stuff to eat along the way. It was a thirty-mile ride, and that would take us at least all day to make it there, you know. My saddled horse was tied on to the rear end of the buggy, in case I should need him, and old Tootie Harman was riding on him with her hands tied to the saddle horn.

Riding up ahead of us, kind of scouting the road ahead, was Texas Jack and Shorty Joe. Riding alongside of us was Scratchy and the Dutchman, one on each side, and taking up the rear was the rest of my posse: Ten-Gallon, Remuda, and Chicago. Every one of us men was armed like we was going into the goddamndest war you ever seen or ever even heard about, and with us like to maybe running into the goddamned Bensons somewheres along the way, that's just exactly how I felt like. I wasn't taking no chances. And I was driving along of two minds. I didn't really want Lillian to be subjected to no violent behavior, being the real and genuine lady that she was, but at the same damn time, a part of me was hoping that them bastards would come riding down the road right smack into us, 'cause we was a strong force there for damn sure. If we was to run into them that way, it would be a big surprise to them, too. That was the other thing. They wouldn't be expecting to see me till they come riding into Asininity.

"Hey, Texas," I yelled out, and I had to call out real loud in order for him to hear my voice above the buggy wheels, horses' hoofs, clattering and clanking and squeaking of leather and all. He heard me, though, and he turned in his saddle to look back at me. "You see any sign of anyone coming along the road?" I called out.

"Nothing," he hollered back at me.

"Barjack," said my darling thing, looking at me with her angelic face, "are you really expecting trouble along the way?"

"I ain't really expecting none, sweetness," I said, "but it pays to be prepared, and I don't want you to worry none about it, 'cause we're ready just in case it does come along. What I mean to say is that even if trouble does come along, it won't be no trouble at all, the way we're fixed up here."

"I'm not afraid," she said, "not with you beside me."

Oh, my God, how them words puffed me up. I think that I must have smiled just a bit and straightened myself up some and give a right smart flick of the reins to pick up the pace somewhat. I felt like a real fancy-Dan dude. I really did. I was thinking how first thing in the morning, at the latest, I would be married up with that fine lady what was riding along beside me in the buggy. Hell, I figured, if we was to get into the county seat in time, we could maybe even get hitched on up that very evening. Then I wouldn't have to stay in no separate hotel room from Lillian that night. That was the mainest reason I had started us out so early in the morning. 'Course, there wasn't no guarantee, traveling with a buggy and all, but I was sure hoping to make pretty good time. Hell, I even resented the time it took for us to stop off and eat our damned lunch, and I guess I kind of hurried everyone along some.

I can tell you, too, that I was watching in all directions at all times, and I frequently asked the boys if they had seen anything. None of us ever did. Well, it was only the thirteenth, and if the Bensons was meaning to hit Asininity on the fifteenth, we was much more likely, I figured, to run into them at the county seat. That would be all right. I'd have not only my own posse, but I'd have old Sheriff Dick Custer and his deputies, however many of them there might be. Them bastard Bensons would find themselves facing a whole damn army, they would. It almost made me chuckle just thinking about it. God, I hoped that they would start a shooting war with us and all of them get their asses blowed all to hell and gone.

Well, as it turned out, we made damn good time, and we even pulled into the county seat just a little before the offices all closed up. I hustled Lillian along with me into the place where they give out the hitching-up licenses, and we got one with no trouble at all. I was kind of amazed all over again at just what a busy little place our county seat really was. I didn't get over there very often. Hell, you couldn't walk across the street and be safe. You had to be dodging horses and wagons and all, and you couldn't even dare to look down to make sure you wasn't stepping in no horse shit. If you'd looked down, you'd most for sure have been rode over by something.

"Where are we going now?" Lillian said as we stepped up on the sidewalk again, me clutching our license real tight.

"I'm taking you over to the hotel," I said, "and then I'm going to have a talk with old Dick Custer and dump off my prisoner on him. Soon as I check in with him, you and me will hunt ourselves up a preacher and show him this here license and get him to hitch us up together right good and proper."

I had already told the boys to take the horses all down to the livery and then meet me in the hotel lobby. Whenever I walked in there with Lillian, I couldn't help thinking about what the hell our own hotel was going to look like whenever we was to get it all done. I told myself that this hotel wasn't nothing to what we'd have right over there in Asininity. Anyhow, I walked over to the desk just as bold as I could be, and I seen that the clerk there was looking kind of nervous. Hell, his lobby was filled up with my posse, all tough looking and with guns sticking out all over them.

"You got enough rooms open for me and this bunch?" I asked him.

"Well, yes, sir," he said, kind of stammering. "I believe so. Actually, just now, we happen to have the entire second floor open."

"Well, let me have it," I told him. "I'm Marshal Barjack from over in Asininity, and these men are all my deputies. I'll ask you to send the bill to the Asininity town council. You got a restaurant and bar attached to this place?"

He pointed to a door in the wall to his right side and said, "Yes, sir. Right through there."

"Good," I said. "We'll be signing the tabs in there to put on our bill to the town council. Now, where can I find me a goddamned preacher?"

He told me, and I signed the book and got me a whole handful of room keys. I made the clerk get someone to haul all our luggage up to the second floor. Lillian had more than any of the rest of us. Most of the boys didn't have nothing but a blanket roll. We went on upstairs, and I put Lillian in the first room we come to, after checking it out to make sure that it was okay. I put my stuff in there with hers too, and then I didn't put no one in the next room nor in the room directly across the hall. I give all the boys rooms on down the way. I told them to eat in the restaurant and have themselves a few drinks, but not to get drunk or

I'd kick their ass. Then I excused myself to Lillian, took over Tootie from Texas Jack, and headed on over to see old Dick Custer.

I didn't find him in his office, which wasn't no surprise to me, as by then it was a little after five. I found him in the pool hall shooting a game and drinking a tall, cold beer. I knew better than to interrupt anyone who's leaning over a pool table and fixing to shoot, so I just stood by real quiet and polite-like and holding on to Tootie by the end of the rope which was tied to her wrists while he damn near run the table. When he finally missed one and stepped back, I stepped in.

"Howdy, Dick," I said, and he looked over at me curious-like.

"Who are you?" he said.

Well, that kind of hurt my feelings more than a little bit, 'cause I thought that I was a pretty well-known feller in those parts, and besides, even though I hadn't been over to the county seat for a spell, I had met old Dick before, and he had ought to have remembered me. I tried to shrug off the insult, though. I sucked in a breath and puffed out my chest, at the same time kind of pulling my coat off to one side to show off my marshal's badge there where it was pinned to my vest.

"I'm Barjack," I said, "town marshal over to Asininity."

"Oh, yeah," he said, trying to act like he recollected, even after he had done showed that he never. "What brings you over this way, Barjack? And who've you got there?"

"Well, Sheriff," I said, on purpose not calling him by his name no more, "I come over for one to get myself hitched."

"Congratulations," he said. "Did you have to bring her along like that?"

"No," I said. "Hell. This here ain't who I'm getting hitched to. This here is another reason I come over here. This is Tootie Harman, the widow of old Gap Tooth Harman what just got killed over by Asininity by Fin Brackett. We think that Tootie was in on it with old Fin. We killed Fin, but we brung Tootie over here to you since it all really happened in your jurisdiction."

Old Dick kind of wrinkled up his whole face like he was trying hard to follow all that, and then he called out to a fellow that was setting off in a corner drinking a beer.

"Melvin," he said, "would you take this lady over to the jail and provide her with accommodations? We'll try to straighten the story all out later. And Melvin, when you lock her up, take that rope off of her."

"Yes, sir," said Melvin, and he took Tootie on out of there. I figured him to be one of old Dick's deputies.

"Now," Dick said to me, "you said you're here to get married? Do I know the lady?"

"I don't expect so," I said. "She come into Asininity on the stage the other day. She's a real fine lady, name of Lillian Fields."

A look come over old Custer's face, but he didn't say nothing. I should have took more note of that look, now that I think back on it, but I never. I just went on talking.

"But that ain't all my business," I said. "There's another official reason I come looking for you first thing on arriving here in town."

The other pool shooter finished running the table just then, and old Dick give him a dollar.

"Let's go sit down," he said. "Cold beer?"

"No, thanks," I said. "When I get done here I'm going to look myself up a preacher and get hitched up tonight. I done got the license. I best not be drinking nothing more than coffee till all the wedding's been took care of."

"We got some of that, too," he said, and he ordered me up a cup. We set down across from each other at a table over by the wall, and I took a sip of coffee. He drained his mug and called for another beer. After he got it, he took a slurp and set it down on the table. "All right," he said, "what's the rest of your business?"

"Well," said I, "I don't know if you'll recall it or not, but some years back I rounded up the whole rustling clan of Bensons. We got old Vance strung up for murder, and the other ones was all sent up for rustling."

"Yeah," he said, rubbing his chin. "I do recollect that incident. That was a damn good job you did back then.

117

Pretty much put an end to all the rustling around these parts. The Bensons was a bad bunch, all right."

"The worst kind," I said. "Well, Little Red and them other three, his brothers or cousins or whatever they are, has all got out of prison just recent, and they sent me a telegram saying that they're coming into Asininity on the fifteenth to kill my ass."

"That's the day after tomorrow," Custer said.

"Yeah, I know," I said. "Well, I figure if they plan to ride into Asininity at high noon on the fifteenth, they'll likely be riding right in here tonight or sometime tomorrow."

"That figures," Custer agreed.

"Now, I don't want to be running the road toward home with them coming up right behind me," I said.

"I can't blame you for that," he said.

"So I thought that maybe you'd get a bunch of deputies together and help me out," I said. "We can brace ourselves up real good and just meet them head on when they ride in here. I got myself seven good men with me right now. With my seven, eight counting me, and what you can get together, them Bensons won't stand a chance."

"Wait just a minute, Barjack," said Custer. "What is it you want me to do? Help you set up an ambush and commit murder on the Bensons?"

"Hell, yes," I said. "They're planning to commit murder on me, and me an officer of the law. Ain't that against the law?"

"I reckon it is," he said, "but what evidence is there of their intent?"

"Evidence of their intent?" I said, echoing his words. "Hell, man, you sound like that damned Peester. I didn't figure you to go talking like no lawyer."

"Barjack," he said, "we can't just go to killing people because of what we think they're fixing to do. I can stop them and have a talk with them, but I can't make a move against them until they've actually broken the law."

"You ain't going to help me till they've killed me. Is that it?" I said, and then I recalled the other part of my little scheme. "Listen," I said, "I think they've done had a part in committing the murder of old Gap Tooth, which, if you recall what I said before, is under your jurisdiction."

"What makes you think that?" he said, leaning in somewhat and perking up his interest.

"I had me old Gap Tooth acting as a deputy and watching the road," I said. "Someone cut him down with a shotgun blast. It was outside of Asininity, so it was under the county jurisdiction. We followed the trail anyhow, you know, while it was still fresh, and we come up on old Fin Brackett, who had run off with Gap Tooth's wife, that's Tootie who you've just had locked up in your jail. It was Fin done the killing, and he resisted arrest and got his own ass killed in the process. But since he was the one who had the woman, we couldn't figure no reason he would have to come back and kill Gap Tooth other than that the two of them, Fin and Tootie, was in cahoots with the Bensons—a sort of advance team, you might say."

"Barjack," Custer said, "that sounds pretty far-fetched to me, and as far as I can tell, the Bensons have done nothing to warrant any action on our part. Not yet. And if you start anything here with your little army of deputies, I'll throw you in my jail. Now, if the Bensons break the law in any way while they're in my jurisdiction, you let me know about it and I'll take care of it. In the meantime, why don't you go on ahead and get hitched and then go home. I don't want a shoot-out in the county seat, and if anything like that happens, I'll be holding you personally responsible for it. You got that?"

Well, that chapped my ass for damned sure. I pulled the hat down tight on my head and stomped out of that poolroom, and just as I stepped out on the board sidewalk, three revolver shots sounded out, and three slugs thumped into the wall just behind my head.

Chapter Thirteen

I fell down flat on my face as fast as I could fall, and as I was a-diving, I heard someone yell out from somewhere out in front of me.

"Barjack, you son of a bitch," he hollered, "we ain't in your goddamned town now."

Old Dick Custer come a-running out of that pool hall with a six-gun in each hand.

"Across the street," he said. "Come on."

He commenced to running and shooting at the same time, and I rolled over a few times as some more shots was coming my way from across the street. Then I scrambled down behind a nearby watering trough, and a bullet hit the front side of it. I hauled out my Merwin and Hulbert Company revolver and peeked real cautious-like up over the edge of the trough. I wondered where all my worthless deputies was at just then, and just then, too, I seen a figure across the street standing in between two buildings and a-blazing away, but just as I spotted him, old Dick took aim and fired a slug right into the son of a bitch's gut. The dry-gulching bastard groaned and slumped and dropped his shooter. He swayed a bit, and then he just kind of slumped over and crumpled into a ball there in the dirt.

"Come on, Barjack," Custer yelled, and he went to running down that dark lane in between the two buildings. "There's one more."

One, hell, I thought. There's four of them bastards. But I stood up and started after Custer. Before I took into that lane, though, I thought better of it. The bastard we was after would come to the end of the lane and then have to turn one way or the other. I went to my right and run around the building there, and about halfway down the side, running toward the back side, I seen him. He come running around the corner from the back, and he still had his iron in his hand. I didn't give it no second thought. I just raised up my revolver and blasted away. I hit him three or four times, I think, and I don't think he ever even seen me. He was too worried about old Custer coming at him from behind. He staggered a bit, then stopped. His hand went limp, and he let his shooter drop. Then he clutched at his chest with both hands, and then he looked up and seen me.

"Barjack," he said, and he fell over dead. Custer come running around the corner then. He stopped when he seen that I had got that one. He holstered his gun and walked over to the stiff. It was laying on its face. He rolled it over with the toe of his boot. "Which one is this?" he asked me.

I walked on over to take a look, and was I surprised. "Why, it ain't none of them," I said. "It's just old Snuff."

"Who?" said Custer.

But I didn't answer him. I was headed back out to the street to take a look at the other one, but I pretty well knowed who it would be then. Custer followed me, and we come on the other one still crumpled up there in a ball. I give him a shove with my boot, and he fell back on his back. He was still gurgling, not quite gone, and he rolled his eyes at me and called me a son of a bitch, and before he died, I said, "Same to you, Dusty."

"Who the hell were they?" Custer said.

"Just a couple of goddamned drifters," I said. "They come through Asininity the other day and got themselves throwed in jail. I reckon they was carrying a grudge over it."

Old Custer called out to someone to come on over and take care of the corpuses derelict, and I let it be knowed that I could sure use a glass of whiskey. "Come on," Custer said. "I'll buy you one." We went into a place just a couple of doors down from where we was at, and we bellied up to the bar. The barkeep come over to see what it was we wanted, and we told him whiskey. He put a bottle and a couple of shot glasses in front of us, but I told him to get me a tumbler, and I poured it about halfway up. I took me a good healthy slug of the stuff and then set my glass back down.

"Barjack," said Custer, "when those two started shooting at you, I thought for sure that it must have been the Bensons. I thought that I was going to have to take back everything I'd said to you."

"Hell," I said, "I thought it was them too. I never figured them two drifters would try anything like that. Dumb-ass bastards."

"Well," Custer said, "I can't rightly go back on what I said before, but if the Bensons show up, I'll hold them off long enough for you to get your wedding done and get started back on the road to Asininity. I'll do that much for you."

I couldn't argue with that. It was more than I expected from him after what he had said to me in the pool hall. I just nodded in a kind of acknowledgment of what he had said, and then I guzzled down some more whiskey. There ain't nothing that makes me want a good hard drink of whiskey like getting shot at. But he had also reminded me of my wedding, which was planned for that very evening and was the whole main reason for the trip over to the county seat in the first place, and here I was drinking whiskey in the goddamned saloon and my darling sweetheart just a-setting over there all by her lonesome in a hotel room. I turned the glass up and drained it.

"Thanks for the drink, Sheriff," I said. I was still burning just a bit from when he didn't recognize me. "I got to go find me a preacher now." I turned around and started to walk off.

"Barjack," Custer kind of snapped out at me. I stopped in my tracks and turned back to look at him, half expecting from the tone of his voice to find myself looking down the barrel of his six-gun, but I wasn't. He was just standing there at the bar and looking at me. "Go down to the north end of the street," he said. "There's a little house with a white picket fence around it on your right-hand side. That's Preacher Harp's house. He'll take care of you."

"Thanks," I said. I didn't bother telling him that the hotel clerk had done told me about that place. I walked on back over to the hotel. Up in the room I give a sincere apology to my lady love and told her what had happened that had made me take so long getting back to her. She hugged my neck and made over me something wonderful. Then, with her sweet help, I straightened myself up a bit, dusted off my duds, and then I rounded up the whole posse for a wedding party.

I guess we like to scared old Preacher Harp into just about pissing his pants when the bunch of us crowded onto his front porch. Lillian was the only one who didn't look like she was going to a killing. The rest of us was still packing our whole damned arsenal. Wedding or no wedding, I still wasn't taking no chances on getting caught out unprepared. I had done been shot at by two drifters and hadn't even seen no Bensons yet. But I told old Harp who I was and why I had my armed men with me, and he understood all right, I reckon.

He didn't invite us into his house, though. He went back inside and come out again a minute later toting his Bible, and we had our wedding right there on his front porch. I made all my deputies take off their hats and hold them till all the words was said, and when the last word was said, Lillian give me a kiss the like of which I had not had from her before. It like to made me faint dead away right there on that preacher's porch, and all the posse hoorawed and waved their hats.

Oh, I was the most thrilled I had ever been in my whole

life. It was almost more than I could believe that I had even met and talked with this vision of delightfulness, that this lady who was so far above me in social status and every other way had even bothered talking to me in the first place and then becoming acquainted with me, but that she had actual agreed to marry up with me, and now she had actual gone and done it—well, Lord God Jesus Christ son of a bitch. There just ain't no way to describe the incredible overwhelming feelings that come dropping down on me standing there on that preaching bastard's porch. And all that while Lillian was holding me in her arms and planting that wondrous kiss on my lips.

Well, then, the boys all pulled out their six-guns and started in to shooting them up in the air and whooping and hollering even more, and Lillian finally let me loose, and I come up for air and sucked in a whole bunch of it, and then I waved my hat in the air too, and I yelled out at the top of my lungs, "Let's go, boys. The drinks is on me," and I give that preacher ten bucks and then led the wedding march back toward the bar in the hotel. I noticed as we was leaving the porch that Preacher Harp looked awful relieved to see us going. Well, all that shooting must have drawed old Dick Custer back out into the street, 'cause when we was about halfway back to the hotel, he met us there. Seeing the sheriff, the boys kind of quieted down. Old Dick looked right at Lillian, and he touched the brim of his big wide black hat and nodded his head.

"Mrs. Barjack?" he said.

Lillian give him a smile. "Yes, Sheriff," she said.

He looked at me then. "Everything go all right?" he asked.

"Slicker'n—well, yeah," I said. "It's all done, and I reckon it took."

"Congratulations," he said. "Uh, you think you could quiet the wedding party down a bit now?"

I looked over my shoulder and said, "You heard the sheriff, boys. Holster them guns." Then I looked back at Custer. "Join us over at the hotel for a drink?" I asked him.

"I reckon that under the circumstances," he said, "it wouldn't hardly be polite to refuse."

He turned and walked along beside of me as we headed on toward the hotel, and just then up ahead of us almost like it was in a dream, I seen four riders coming slow right toward us. They was like a silhouette, or rather four silhouettes, and they seemed to be moving unnatural slow and weird-like. I felt a clammy chill clamp over my whole body, and at the same time I could feel beads of sweat pop out on my forehead. I stopped walking, and so did the rest of the group. I guess we all just stared straight ahead a-waiting for the four eerie-looking figures to get close enough for us to see just who the hell they was. But I didn't need to wait. I knowed it was the Bensons. The happiest moment of my whole entire life had just been rudely interrupted by the scardiest one. Finally they hove on up and drawed in their mounts just right there in front of us, not more than five or six feet away. I seen all their faces clear, and they seen me too. Little Red grinned real wide, and I could see where he still had some few of his nasty yellow teeth.

"Well, howdy, Barjack," he said. "We sure wasn't expecting to see you over here."

Custer looked at me out of the corners of his eyes. "Bensons?" he asked me in a low voice.

"It's them, all right," I said.

"Who's the lady?" Little Red asked.

"It's the brand-spanking-new Mrs. Barjack," I said. "This here's a wedding-party, and I don't want no trouble from you Benson bastards here tonight."

"I don't want no trouble at all here in my town," said Custer, his voice booming out big and making me a little ashamed of my piping tone. "I know why you boys are here, but if you start anything here, I promise you that I'll finish it."

"Why, Sheriff," Little Red said, "we didn't come here to cause no trouble. And we sure don't want to interfere with old Barjack's wedding night. We'll just have us a few drinks and then move on. We're just passing through anyway."

"Where you moving on to?" Custer asked.

"We're headed for Asininity, Sheriff," Little Red said. "We got us an appointment, you might say, for the fifteenth. High noon."

Chapter Fourteen

Well, there was, like they say, a moment of silence. Then I seen a man come off the sidewalk and walk real quiet-like up behind the Bensons. He looked to me to be carrying a scattergun. I'm sure that all of us seen him, but I'm just as sure that he total sneaked up on them Bensons. Old Dick Custer reached over and put a hand on my back and give a gentle shove.

"Barjack," he said, "why don't you take your party on over to the hotel." I started to protest, but he stopped me. "Go on," he said. "All of you. Have a good time. I'll take care of this."

Little Red laughed. "Yeah, Barjack," he said. "Have yourself a real good time. Hell, we might just come on over and have us a drink with you and your bride to help you celebrate the happy occasion."

"Shut up, Benson," Custer said, and he drawed his revolver out, just slow and casual, like he wasn't worried about nothing at all.

"You heard the sheriff," I said, taking Lillian by the arm. "Let's go." I headed for the hotel, and my whole wedding party went along with me, but I kept craning my neck to see what was happening back there with Custer and the Bensons. I thought, I hope he pisses them off as bad as I did, so they can't figure out which one of us they wants to kill the worst. Custer had his gun out, and Little Red just laughed at him.

"You boys shuck your weapons," Custer said. "There's a shotgun right behind you."

The last I seen of them was Custer and his deputy with the shotgun marching them four Bensons toward his jailhouse. I breathed a heavy sigh of great relief, but I knowed it was just only temporary. Old Custer had said that he'd hold them up for me for a while. That's all. I was still going to have to deal with them. No doubt about that. No question at all. I tried my damndest to stand tall with my chest out and hold my head up and keep a brave face, but I ain't sure that I done a very good job of it. Anyhow we all got back over to the hotel and on into the room what served as a restaurant and a bar, and we ordered drinks all around. By and by, Custer come in.

I had a tumbler of whiskey on the table in front of me, and Lillian, setting beside me, was sipping champagne. Some of the boys was setting at tables and some was bellied up to the bar. They was all drinking whiskey. I got a glass of whiskey for Custer, and he set down at the table with me and Lillian. I can tell you that my festive mood of earlier in the evening was done gone. The sight of them Bensons had blowed it clean away. I was sure grateful to old Custer, though, for giving me at least one more night to live on this earth.

"I locked them up," Custer said. "I'll keep them in there until you've had time tomorrow to get well on your way back home. From there on, it's your problem."

"Thanks—Dick," I said. I was racking my brain, doing some painful thinking, Texas Jack–style, trying to come up with some reason old Custer might could have to hold them Bensons longer than what he said, or some reason why they had ought to go back to the pen, or better yet, some way to just get them all killed. I considered sending Texas Jack over to the jailhouse in the deep middle of the night to just shoot the four bastards through the window of their cell, but then I was afraid that he wouldn't do no cold-blooded quadruple murder for me, even considering how much he owed to me and all. I thought then about doing the dastardly deed my own self, but I pondered all the variables that would be involved in such a deal. I'd have to climb up on something to get a good look into the cell, and then I'd have to shoot them down one at a time. And I might not kill one or more of them right off with just only one shot, shooting through the bars and in the dark like that. It might take more than four shots to do it right.

Four shots or more ringing out like that in the middle of the night was bound to rouse up old Custer, and he just might come a-running before I was done with the job or at least before I would be able to get myself clean away from the scene of the mayhem. And even if I was to get away clean, he would surely come looking for me first thing. There wasn't no one else in the whole goddamned world that wanted the Bensons dead worse than what I did, and he knowed it. Well, my analyzing of the possible outcome of the plan kept leading up to one main result, which was that old Dick Custer would either shoot my ass or throw it in jail, and in that last of the two, I would wind up getting my neck stretched. I didn't have no interest in that kind of unpleasantness. I would much ruther, of the two, let the Bensons shoot me down.

Well, the best I could think, there wasn't a goddamned thing that I could be doing about my precarious situation except only what I was already doing, and that was doing nothing about it at all. All I could do was only to just wait out the night and lead my wedding party back to Asininity in the morning, knowing all the while that the Bensons would be coming along behind us. They wouldn't be too close on our tail, though, 'cause old Custer had done promised me that he would hold them up for a spell there in his jailhouse, but they'd be coming along, sooner or later. I took another gulp of whiskey, and then it come to me that I could still make use of my original plan.

And at this point Old Custer was cooperating with it too. Maybe he knowed it and maybe he didn't, but that didn't matter none. He was going to give me a good head start and then turn them bastards loose. Hell, I had me and six more with enough guns amongst us for twenty or so. We could move on down the road a ways and then lay up an ambush and just wait for them four bastards and then whenever they come along, why, just shoot them all full of holes until they was all leaking like sieves. There wouldn't be nothing to it. At least, there shouldn't be. Once I come up with that thought, I relaxed a little bit. In fact, it kind of tickled me to know that Custer was helping it along. Just then old Texas Jack broke in real loud on everyone's thoughts, including mine. He had been bellied up to the bar, and he turned around wobbling somewhat and held his glass up real high, sloshing out some whiskey in the process.

"Here's to the marshal's lady," he shouted, and the others all hollered out, "Hear, hear." The Dutchman stood up then from where he was setting and raised up his glass in response to all that. "May they have a long and happy life together," he said.

Scratchy called out then, "And lots of little fat kids."

All kinds of laughing and hoorawing followed that, but that last comment had kind of set me back a bit. Hell, I had not ever even thought about no little fat kids, but I reckoned that it was bound to happen one of these days. Then even old Dick Custer raised up his glass, but he never stood up and he didn't holler out loud. Instead he just looked right straight at Lillian in the face and he said, "I wish you a long and happy life." Well, there was something in his look that I didn't like, and I recalled the look that had come over his face when I had first mentioned her name to him. I had kind of let that one pass, but this time it set in my brain real good. There was something going on there that commenced to worrying me, but what could I say? Just that old Dick Custer had got a funny look on his face two times, and both times it had to do with my wife.

Why, someone might answer me that old Dick looked funny all the damn time. Or they might say that old Dick was trying to figure out why a beat-up old son of a bitch such as I was ever come up with such a marvel of delight as what I had got ahold of for myself in that lovely lady Lillian. I told myself that must be it. He was wondering about my miraculous good fortune. That was a comforting thought under the circumstances, and besides, I had too many other things to worry about just then, and they was life-and-death things. It come to me about then that by rights I had ought to go upstairs with my new bride and get the two of us on into our wedding bed. That thought made me flush hot, I can tell you.

With old Bonnie I could always just say, "Let's go upstairs," and she would go on along with me, knowing right away what it was that was on my mind, but I for sure couldn't be that blunt with a fine lady like Lillian, and that right there in front of other folks. I was trying to figure out just how to lay the hint on her and get us the hell on out of that bar and up the stairs, when old Texas raised up his glass again and give a loud hooraw and then fell over flat on his face. That boy never could hold his liquor. Custer give me a look.

"He'll be all right come morning," I said. Custer give a shrug. Then Lillian took the last sip out of her glass, and she done it so delicate that it just give me goose bumps all over to see it. Then she looked at me real sweet and lovely, and she said, "Don't you think that it's time we retired to our room?" Godalmighty, that just made me quiver, and I stood right up and moved around behind her chair to pull it back a little and let her stand up. I hadn't had much practice, but I did know how to act like a gentleman. "Will you excuse us, Sheriff Custer?" she said.

Old Dick stood up like as if to show me that I wasn't the only one who knowed how to behave in front of a lady, and he said, "By all means, Mrs. Barjack." I liked the sound of her being called that. I picked up my hat and waved it and called out, "Good night, boys," and I picked up my glass and the whiskey bottle too. I almost walked on out like that, but I give it another quick thought and picked up Lillian's glass and the champagne bottle too, and I give old Custer a wink and walked out of there with my lady love hanging on to my arm. The last thing I noticed was Remuda and Chicago moving over to set down with old Custer. I guessed that all the boys would all have themselves a real good time for most of the rest of that night, but it wouldn't be nothing to the good time that I was anticipating upstairs with my lovely lady.

Me and Lillian strolled on through the lobby of the hotel just like we was fine folks, and then we headed on up the stairs, her still hanging on to my arm, and as we started to take them steps, I noticed that I was feeling my whiskey just a little bit. I figured that was all right, though. Being just a little heady like that wasn't nothing to worry about in view of what I fixing to be up to. In fact, I always found it to be somewhat desired. We made the top of the stairs and walked over to the door to our room, and I went to reach for the key, but I couldn't get to it with my arms and my hands all full of bottles and glasses the way they was, and Lillian still hanging on to my one arm, too. She saw how I was fumbling around, and she knowed why, and she giggled about it.

"Where is it?" she asked me.

I told her which pocket the key was in, and she reached right in there for it. She unlocked the door, and we went on inside. I put down all the bottles and glasses, and I turned to look at her. I was nervous and a little bit embarrassed. I had been bragging to myself that I knowed how to act the gentleman, but not until just that very minute had I asked myself how a gentleman behaves with a lady under these very special circumstances. But Lillian come to the rescue again. She give me a kind of coy look, and she took off her hat and laid it aside, and then she let her hair down and give it a shake-out. God, I trembled. I did recall, though, even in the state I was in, how I had caught up old Vance Benson all them years ago, and I went and locked the door.

When I turned back around, I seen that Lillian was already taking off her clothes. Well, there was a big moon out that night, and the room was dark, but it was lit just a little by the moonlight coming in through the window, and I could see her outlined in that light, and my God, it was a lovely sight to behold. I felt like I had died and gone to heaven and been met there by an angel of heavenly divinity, but I knowed that was only just a fantasy, 'cause considering the life I had led, if I was actual dead I for sure wouldn't be in the company of no angel. Most likely I'd be surrounded by little red grinning imps with pitchforks.

So I knowed it was real. It was me and it was Lillian and we was man and wife. What's more, it was our wedding night, and we was alone in a hotel room, and she had just got herself naked as a newborn babe. I started in pulling off my own clothes then. I didn't want to waste no more of this precious time. After all, even with my well-laid plans, it was just possible that this here could be my last night on earth, and I figured that this was sure as hell the best possible way to spend it. By the time I had stripped off the last of my duds, Lillian was already laying on the bed with the covers all shoved down to the foot. She was laying there all uncovered and inviting, and I moved right on over there and crawled myself in right beside her, and we snuggled up and hugged each other real tight and close. The feel of her delightful flesh all up and down and against my own bare skin was almost more than I could stand, and I assure you that I wasn't no neophyte. And then she kissed me, long and deep, and I was moaning out loud it was so good. If I had to get myself killed stone dead the very next day, I told myself, I wouldn't mind it so much after all.

Chapter Fifteen

Well, by Godfrey damn, it had never happened to me before in my whole entire long life of adventures, wicked and otherwise. It was a total brand-new and genuine shocking experience for me, and it was the single worst misfortune of my life, worse even than waking up without my boots and hats and guns and money that one time. In fact, I couldn't think of nothing worse having ever befell on me, not even coming up on the Bensons alone and unarmed. I even got to thinking that the best thing that could happen to me at that point would be if the goddamned Bensons was to go on ahead and kill me deader'n hell, for I sure as hell felt like I wanted to be dead. There I was, alone with my new sweet wife on our very wedding night, and her the most loveliest of visions I had ever seen in my whole entire life, the most sweetest and most desirable woman I had ever knowed, hell, ever even imagined that I would ever know. There we was with everything legal and proper and decent about the situation, and I couldn't do it. Me!

I couldn't—well, you know what I mean. It's so god-awful embarrassing, I don't like to recall it even now. I don't like putting words to it. It pains me and grieves me to the quick. To say that I was disappointed in my own self would be the understatement of the centuries. It would miss the mark by at least a hundred million, way more higher than I can count. I was embarrassed. Hell, I was humiliated. My face was burning red. I could feel it. I could think of only one good thing about the situation I was in, and that was that it was dark in the room and Lillian couldn't see my face in the moment of my monumental dishonor. I thought that she could never again have no love nor even respect for me. She wouldn't even be able to think that I was a real man no more. How could she, for I wasn't so sure about that myself no more. I kept asking myself what I had ever done in my whole, entire, long, and eventful life to deserve such a miserable fate as that what I was suffering. I done some bad things. I knowed that, but I could not convince myself that I ever done anything to bring this disaster on myself. Well, no one ever told me that life was fair and just, and I never had no better evidence of that fact than what I had right then.

I started to get up and get dressed and excuse myself and go on downstairs and just get drunk with the boys, but then I realized that if I was to do that, they'd all know that something had went wrong. Hell, there wasn't nothing I could do. Staying there in the room with Lillian, who knowed firsthand about my damn near unmentionable shame, was pure torture, but showing myself outside of the room to men who knowed damn well what it was I was supposed to be doing would be even worse. I tell you, boys, I was strapped.

"Maybe you had a little too much to drink," Lillian said, and her voice was still sweet. I got to hand it to her. She didn't give me no hard time for what I had failed to do.

"It ain't the whiskey," I said, standing up nekkid to pour myself a drink. "Hell, I've drank lots more than that, and still—well, it just ain't the whiskey. That's all."

"Barjack," she said, "come on back to bed and let me hold you. It's all right. Really it is. You've been shot at today, and you had to kill a man. Then those other four showed up. Those Bensons. Why, it's more than enough to put any man down. Come on over here to me now. Come on."

Her words was sweet, and they helped some, but not enough, I can tell you. Still, I couldn't resist her. I gulped down the drink I had just poured, and then I done what she had just told me to do. I went on back over there and laid down beside her on my bed of shame, and she just took ahold of my head and laid it right down on her lovely tit. Oh, God, how I hated myself for not being able to do my manly duty on that beautiful and sweet woman. I was also praying that no one would ever find out anything about this horrible night, that it would stay a secret between just me and Lillian. I couldn't stand the thought of being laughed at over this terrible thing that had happened to me.

'Course, I knowed that Lillian was every inch a lady and wouldn't never speak about it to anyone. Still there was something inside of me nagging at me and telling me that I could become a laughingstock over this thing, and I was asking myself is there any way that the word could get out? I even wondered if I should shake the bed back and forth to make it sound like something was really going on in that room, but then I remembered that I had made sure there wouldn't be nobody in any of the nearby rooms anyway. There wouldn't be no one around to wonder why they wasn't hearing no telltale noises.

Well, I can tell you that I tried every trick I could think of, and even Lillian surprised the hell out of me by trying some pretty bizarre things herself on me, but nothing neither one of us could do made no difference. I just stayed totally useless that whole damn night. Well, since I couldn't do nothing else, I just kept on drinking whiskey, and by and by, mercifully, I guess I just kind of passed out. It was a hell of a sorry wedding night. One that I'd never forget, and neither, I'm sure, would Lillian. That's for damn sure.

August 14

Well, I woke up, or come to, whichever one you want to call it, kind of late the next morning, and Lillian was already up and dressed and looking just as beautiful as ever, and even acting just as pleasant, too. I was kind of embarrassed, given my poor performance of the night before, to get out of bed stark naked like that, her standing in the room all dressed, but I didn't have no choice. I had to get out of bed in order to get to my clothes and put them on. So I did, but my face was burning red. My shoulders was slumped, too, and my head was hanging in shame. It wasn't the only thing.

"Good morning, darling," Lillian said to me in that wonderful musical voice of hers. Hell, I was too ashamed to even answer her. I had pulled on my britches and was just about to button up my shirt. She stepped up to me and put her arms around my neck and give me a sweet kiss on the cheek. "It's all right," she said. "Believe me. There will be other nights. Lots of them."

I finally found my voice. "Lillian," I said, "I feel the awfullest that I've ever felt in my life, and I guess I couldn't stand it at all, if you wasn't being so good about it. I don't know what I ever done to deserve anyone as wonderful as what you are."

"Hush," she said. "Finish getting dressed, and let's go down and have ourselves some breakfast. We'll be proud and happy, and no one will ever know that things didn't go—well, just as they should have gone up here last night."

Well, I done like she said, and I studied myself in the mirror. At first I thought that it showed all over me just what kind of night I'd had, but then I told myself that was a bunch of bunk. I forced myself to stand up straight and suck in my gut and puff out my chest. I tilted my head back just a little bit, and I set my hat on top just a little jaunty. I strapped on my six-guns and then cocked my left arm out to one side and offered it to Lillian. "Let's go," I said. She took my arm and smiled, and we left the room and headed down to the restaurant.

Because of the time of morning, there wasn't very many customers in there, and the only one of my bunch that we seen was old Texas. I figured that he had passed out so early the night before that he'd had plenty of time to sleep it off. He was setting at a table all by his lonesome, so me and Lillian went and joined him there. He looked up and kind of grinned. "Morning, Marshal," he said. "Ma'am."

"How's your head, Texas?" I said.

"Aw, it ain't bad," he said. "Anyhow, it was worth it."

"You seen any of the other boys?" I asked him.

"Remuda and Chicago was in here just finishing up their breakfasts when I come in," he said. "We had us a little visit, and then they went on outside, I guess. I ain't seen none of the rest of them."

A waiter came and took our breakfast orders. He left again and come back pretty quick with some coffee for us. Texas had done ordered, so he got his meal before we did. He looked a little bit like he didn't know what to do, being the only one at the table with anything to eat. Like she most always done, Lillian rescued him from his predicament.

"Go ahead and eat, please," she said. "Ours will be along soon enough."

Well, old Texas never had to be told twice to eat. He dug right in. He was about halfway through all them eggs and taters when Scratchy and the Dutchman come in, so that only left Ten-Gallon, and Shorty Joe was unaccounted for. I figured they was still sleeping it off and would likely be down pretty soon. Texas finished up his meal and made like he was ready to go, so I give him something to do.

"Run over to the jailhouse," I said, "and make damn sure them four Bensons is still locked up tight. If you see old Dick Custer over there, tell him we're fixing to pull out just as soon as everyone has ate."

"Okay, Marshal," he said, and he took on out of there. Right after that the waiter come back and brought our breakfasts to me and Lillian. Shorty Joe and Ten-Gallon come in about then and set down. Scratchy and the Dutchman had done ordered. I seen them.

"It won't be long now," I said to Lillian. "We'll be on our way home."

I was thinking that once we got home and had them Bensons out of the way, I'd be able to have myself a proper wedding night with Lillian there in our house on the edge of Asininity. 'Course, I was also thinking about the getting rid of them four bastards. I didn't have no way of knowing just how long old Custer would hang on to them assholes for me, but he had said that he'd give us a good start. I was still thinking about my ambush plan, and it still seemed like the best idea I had came up with ever since I had got that goddamned telegram. I hadn't said nothing about it to none of the boys yet, but I figured they'd all go along with it. Hell, if I had to, I'd tell them like I told old Peester. I'd say that whenever they rode into our trap I'd call out to them to surrender, and then if they did, why, we'd just haul their ass on into jail. If they was to resist arrest, we'd have to have us a shooting war with them, and we pretty well outnumbered them. Laying in ambush the way we'd be, we'd already all of us have our guns out and ready too. 'Course, I also figured that I would likely fire the first shot. I figured once the shooting got to going hot and heavy, no one would remember, if he ever even noticed in the first place, who it was who done that.

With my mind well set on my plan, just as soon as Scratchy and the Dutchman had finished their meals, I motioned old Scratchy over to our table where me and Lillian was sipping on refills of our coffee. I told him to start rounding up the boys and to go on over to the stable and get our horses all ready to go. Texas come back in just then.

"They're locked up tight all right," he said. "Miz Harman too, and I told the sheriff we'd be hauling it on out of here pretty soon now."

"Good," I said, and I noticed that he was eyeballing Lillian somewhat strange. The way that he looked at her, I couldn't put no meaning to it, but I didn't like it none. I decided to run him off again. "Go tell that clerk out there to get all our stuff all hauled down out of our rooms," I said. "Tell him to get the bill ready for me to sign, too. Soon as them last two boys finishes eating, we'll be on our way."

Chapter Sixteen

We was all mounted up and ready to go. Me and my wife was in the buggy, me holding the reins, of course, and I was all set to flick the reins and cluck at the old gray mare, when I seen old Dick Custer coming our way and Tootie Harman walking along beside him. I set there and waited on him, and whenever he come up close to the buggy, he pulled off his hat and nodded at Lillian.

"Morning, Miz Barjack," he said, and once again I thought that I seen something in his face that I didn't like, and I looked real quick-like over at Lillian, but she looked just as pleasant and as nice as could be.

"Good morning, Sheriff Custer," she said.

"I trust you had a pleasant night," he said, the son of a bitch. I could have killed him dead whenever he said that, but I just gritted my teeth real hard and set there. Then he said to me, "Barjack, I'll hold those Bensons till you've had time to get halfway back to Asininity. That's about the best I can do for you."

Well, I'm just as sure as hell it was the very best the bastard could do. Why, if the situation had been reversed,

I bet you I could have held whoever it was that was after old Dick for a month or even till hell was to freeze over, if I was a mind to, but he was just about as bad as old Peester about the goddamned law books. "Thanks, Dick," I said, but I was burning hot under my skin, and I really wanted to tell him just what I thought about his sissy notions of law and order and such. 'Course, if I had gone ahead and done that, I might have pissed him off so much that he might have just gone right on over to the jailhouse and turned them bastards loose on me right then. I knowed that, and that's why I kept my real, true thoughts to myself.

"But I can't find a reason to hold Mrs. Harman," the sheriff continued on, "and since you brought her over here against her will, I suggest you take her back home."

Tootie looked at me and said, "Asshole."

"Shove her up on my horse there," I said, and he did. Then I clucked at the old gray mare and flicked the reins and we started off with a lurch. I couldn't help myself. I glanced over at the jailhouse as we drove by it. I knowed who all was in there and what they was thinking about doing to me when they got out. Well, by God, I'd have a right surprise a-waiting for them when they come on to do it. I'd get their ass all killed proper, and then I could get down to the real important things in life, the fixing up of my hotel and restaurant, and the shaping up of my ranch.

The street was busy as usual, and I really had to watch myself to keep from running into other buggies and wagons or running over pedestrians, but I was weaving my way pretty good through all that traffic when I happened to notice off to one side a sign on a storefront that caught my eye. I hauled back on the reins and stopped my whole damned entourage. "DYNAMITE," it said. By God, of a sudden, I wanted some of that. Nothing else was going my way, and I figured that if I lived through the Bensons' visit, I'd blow that stream out on my ranch.

I told everyone to wait up for just a minute or two while I ran in the store and made a purchase. It was a hardware store, and the man inside was busy with a few customers, but eventual he got around to me, and I told him what I wanted. He give me a right curious look, but I just stared back at him real hard. I told him I wanted a few sticks of the stuff, and I said that he could bill the town council of Asininity for it. I showed him my badge and identified myself to him by name. He balked some, but I badgered him into it. Then I signed his bill and I tucked them sticks inside of my coat, and then I bought myself a real expensive cigar. I went on back outside, climbed up into the buggy, and then we started off again.

"Barjack," Lillian said, "what did you go in there for?"

"What?" I said, acting real innocent like. I figured I'd surprise her when I started in to working on the ranch.

"That store," she said. "Why did you go in there?"

"Oh, that," I said. I reached into my pocket and pulled out my cigar. I stuck it in my mouth. "I just realized that I was clean out of these things. I might want one before we get back home. That's all."

Well, I don't believe for a minute that she bought that line, but she didn't say nothing more about it. She just give me a kind of a look, you know.

Just as soon as we got on out of town on the road to Asininity, there wasn't no more traffic, not hardly a sign of life other than just our own selfs. Hell, no one hardly ever went into Asininity on purpose, just only the farmers and cowboys who lived closer to there than to the county seat. They come in mostly to drink or gamble or whore. If they wanted to buy something, they'd usually go on farther on over to the county seat. If they was in a real hurry to get something, they'd come into the store there in Asininity, but the price was always higher there, so mostly they went on over to the county seat.

We rode on for quite a spell not saying nothing, and I was still thinking about when the Bensons would be coming along, and about my shameful night the night before. I figured that Lillian, as good as she was, was thinking about that too. It wasn't the kind of thing you forget very easy. Tootie was talking to Ten-Gallon, who had rode up beside her, and some of the boys following along was talking to each other and laughing a little, at jokes or something, I guess, and I noticed that old Texas seemed to be getting pretty chummy with Remuda and Chicago. Well, we was damn near to the halfway mark, and I was thinking about stopping for a rest and a lunch break,'cause old Dick Custer was likely turning them Bensons loose just about then, when I seen about a dozen riders coming at us from across the open prairie at an angle that would have had them coming from kind of west of Asininity. At first I thought that maybe they was some of the boys coming to help out in case of the Bensons arriving early. When they come closer I could see for sure that it was old Hardass Taylor, the owner of the ranch that Shorty Joe and them come off of. I called a halt to my posse, and pretty soon old Hardass stopped himself and all his men right there in the road in front of us.

"Howdy, Hardass," I said, "what brings you and all that bunch out this way? You bringing me some reinforcements? We can sure use them. The Bensons is over at the county seat right now."

"To hell with the Bensons and you," he said.

"But we seen them over there last night," I told him.

"I come after my boys," he said. "I need them back at the ranch."

"What do you mean by that?" I asked him. "Didn't you hear what I just said? The Bensons is coming. Four of them. They're right behind us right now."

"My four cowboys," he said, just ignoring all my words. "I got need of them."

"Hell," I said, "they're my deputies now, duly sworn. I got need of them too, so I reckon you're just out of luck."

"They work for me, Barjack," Hardass said, "and I mean to take them back to the ranch, and that right now. Come on, boys, if you want to keep your jobs."

Well, them four rode right on up beside the buggy.

"You bastards stay right here," I said. "You ain't released from posse duty. Hardass, you can't interfere with the business of the law."

"Barjack," Hardass said, "you try to interfere with the

business of my ranch, and you'll wish you was facing the Bensons 'stead of me and my crew."

"Marshal," Shorty Joe said, "this here posse ain't going to last longer than tomorrow afternoon. Our jobs with Mr. Taylor is permanent. Sorry, but I'm going back to the ranch."

"Me too," said Chicago. "See you around, I hope."

"Ten-Gallon?" I said as he nudged his horse forward. "You playing out on me too?"

"I got to go where the steady work is," he said.

Remuda touched the brim of his hat as he rode past me. Then old Hardass whipped his horse around and started riding off across country, and the rest of them cowhands, including my four just former deputies, rode after him.

"So long, boys," said old Texas, and he just sounded right friendly like everything was fine and dandy. He really pissed me off.

"Goddamn you, Hardass," I shouted as him and his boys kicked up a cloud of dust that rolled back to overwhelm our eyes and lungs. "I'll get you for this." Then I muttered kind of to myself, "If I live long enough." Hell, all of a sudden my hellacious posse was down to just three men, four counting my own self. Four. And there was four Bensons. That would make for an even fight, and I never did believe in giving no one an even break or a fair fight. I was damn near ready to fly into a panic, but I didn't want my Lillian to see none of that. She'd done seen enough, more than enough, of my worse side to last her a lifetime. I tried to calm myself down.

Texas Jack, the Dutchman, and old Scratchy had rode up beside the buggy by then, and I could see that they was looking more than a little bit worried. There we was, the four of us and Lillian, out in the middle of the wide-open prairie feeling mighty little and stark naked, with four of the meanest ass-killers in the whole Wild West coming up behind us. Well, I didn't want to eat the dust of old Hardass and his sorry-ass crew, so I called for a rest right then and there, and we all had our lunch. By the time that was done, the dust had settled, and so we started out again. I told my tiny posse to keep watching our back trail, but nobody seen nobody coming up behind us, and along toward evening we had made it all the way to the rocks where I had posted my guards earlier, there where old Gap Tooth had bought the farm. We still hadn't seen no sign of the Bensons coming along, so I reckoned that old Dick had kept his word all right.

I thought about dropping off a guard there at the rocks, but then I recollected how no one had wanted to stay out there by his lonesome after what had happened to Gap Tooth, and I sure didn't want to ride on into Asininity with only just one deputy along with me. I did kind of grudging-like offer to escort Tootie back out to the Harman place, but she said there wasn't nothing out there, and she'd just as soon go on to town. She said she'd find herself someplace to stay. I didn't say nothing more then, as we rode on through them rocks and back into town. The sun was low when we got to my house. I told the posse to go on to the office and I'd meet them there a little later. They all rode on ahead. I don't know where old Tootie went. Then I escorted Lillian on into the house. We was just standing there in the middle of the living room kind of awkward-like.

"I got to go on down to my marshal's office and meet the boys," I finally said. "Them Bensons could be coming along just any minute now, and when the shooting starts, I sure don't want to be nowhere near you. You'll be safe enough here. They don't know nothing about this house." It come over me then that Lillian's first night as Mrs. Barjack had been a total disaster, and now for her second night, here I was leaving her alone in our new house. "This here ugly business will be all over tomorrow," I said. "Then things'll be different. I promise you that."

"I know they will, Barjack," she said, and she give me a wonderful sweet kiss. I pulled myself away from her and drove on over to the office. I sudden wanted to stay close with my three deputies, so I figured old Porkbarrel could just come on down and fetch back his own damn mare and buggy if he was in a hurry to get them back. The boys was just setting there, sullen and quiet. I went on back around behind my desk, set down, and pulled open a drawer. I leaned way over so that they wouldn't see me slip them blow sticks out from under my coat and put them in the drawer. I wasn't in the mood to answer no questions about them. Then I hauled the whiskey bottle and some glasses out of that same drawer and poured four glasses full. Texas looked out the window and seen Porkbarrel coming along.

"I reckon he's come after his buggy and mare," he said.

Porkbarrel poked his nose into the office.

"You can take it on back now," I said. "Send me the bill."

He grumbled and went on out.

"Help yourselfs, boys," I said, and I picked up the fullest of the four glasses off the top of my desk and took me a healthy slug. The boys all moved up to get theirs.

"What're we going to do, Barjack?" Scratchy said.

"What do you mean?" I answered him.

"I mean, we had a pretty damn strong posse up till now," Scratchy said, "but now look at us. It's just us. Just the four of us right here in this little room. And them Bensons coming in to town tomorrow. What're we going to do?"

"There's four of them and four of us," I said, knowing full well that I didn't like them odds either, but trying to act like that meant it wasn't no problem. "We're all well armed, and we're ready for them. What's wrong with that?"

"I—well, I don't like it," said Scratchy. "It ain't like it was earlier when there was more of us. Them Bensons is real tough characters. Barjack, they're only coming in here just to kill you. That's all they want, ain't it? Well, why don't you just get yourself on out of town? We won't tell them which way you rode out. Hell, we'll even point them in the wrong direction for you. They'll head out of here after you, but going the wrong way, and everything'll be all right. You'll be safe. We'll all be safe. What do you say?"

"Scratchy," I said, "I got myself a job and a business in this here town, a ranch just outside of it, I just bought two more pieces of town property, and I got me a new wife. You expect me to leave all that behind and take my wife along with me running out across the prairie like some damn kind of fugitive? Or you think I should just leave her here along with everything else? Is that what you think? Goddamn it, I can't just up and leave here, Scratchy."

"You could come back later when it's safe again," the little chicken said.

"I can't do it," I said.

Scratchy took off the gunbelt that we had issued him and dropped it on my desk. He looked right at me, right the hell in my eyes.

"What the hell are you doing?" I said.

"I'm quitting, Barjack," he said. "I don't mean to get myself killed. If you don't like the odds, you can always get out of town."

Then, by God, he turned and went right out the door, and all I done was just stare after him. The Dutchman and old Texas just kind of sat there stunned-like. Finally Texas tipped up his glass and took a drink.

"Well, Marshal," he said, "it looks like it's just the three of us now."

Chapter Seventeen

So there it was. For certain, it was just the three of us. Three. After all the planning and all the work I had did. It like to made me sick to think on it. Well, by damn, I had to have me another drink of whiskey on that one. There just wasn't nothing else to do. I poured my old tumbler full too. I noticed then that old Texas and the damned Dutchman was just kind of sipping at theirs, but I had me way too much worrying of my own to do to give much of a shit about that. Three of us was all. Just only three of us left. And it was a funny feeling, too. It was just almost like as if I had went into battle with a small army behind me, and then I had came back out of the fight with my troops most nearly wiped out. The only thing is, we hadn't even yet got to the battle site. We hadn't had the fight yet. And them four goddamn Bensons was still on their way to town.

"What the hell is the date?" I said. I had already begun to feel just a bit woozy.

"It's the fourteenth," the Dutchman said. "Of August. Eighteen hundred and eighty-nine."

"To hell with you, Dutchman," I said. "I know the goddamn month and the year. You don't need to tell me that part of it."

"Tomorrow's going to be the fifteenth," Texas added.

"Now, goddamn it, Texas," I said, "if today's the four-teenth, do you really think that I need you to tell me that tomorrow's going to be the fifteenth?"

"Well," he said, "I just—"

"I know what you just, you dumb ass," I said, and I gulped down some whiskey. I thought that it was plenty bad enough that I was fixing to get myself killed without I had to put up with two goddamned dummies in my last precious hours. "Hell," I said. "We got to find us some more men somewheres."

"We come up with all we could think of the first time through," Texas said. "I wrote them all down on that list. Remember? I don't see how we can come up with no more, not at this late date."

"Stop talking about the date," I said, and I gulped some more whiskey down. "Of course I remember. Hell, there's got to be some more. Somewhere. There's got to be. We never had the whole entire local male population in that damn posse, did we?"

"Well, no, we never," said Texas, "but—"

"There's got to be some more goddamn men around here somewheres who can shoot guns and ain't chicken sons of bitches," I said. I lifted my glass to drink some more of that wonderful brown stuff, but by then it was sure mud-dying my thoughts all right. I just kept saying, to myself, More men, more men, but I sure as hell wasn't coming up with no names.

"Marshal?" said Texas. "At a time like this, don't you think that—well, hadn't you oughta be home with Miz Bar-jack?"

I looked up at Texas a-glaring like I most wanted to bash in his brains, 'cept only I knowed that he didn't have any, and so I just only stared hard at him for maybe a couple of minutes or so. Then, talking through my clenched teeth, I said, "You goddamn right I oughta. I surely oughta. She's my brand-spanking-new wife, and I damn well oughta be home with her, but I got these four sons of bitches coming to town by high noon tomorrow with not a damn thing on their minds but just to kill me, and they might could show up early, too, for all I know. I got to be watching out for them, now, don't I? And whenever they do show up, I damn sure don't want them bastards finding me anywhere near her."

"Oh," said Texas. "Yeah. I get it."

I drank some more whiskey then, and I made like I was glaring at old Texas some more, but only what I was really doing was I was staring at two fuzzy images and both of them was him, and they wasn't standing still, neither. I know I drank some more after that, and I remember that things just seemed to get more fuzzier and stupider looking, and the room commenced to moving around real slow-like, and the floor begun to tilting back and forth on me, and I guess I kind of passed out soon after that.

August 15
The Day of Reckoning
Is Come at Last

When I eventual raised my head up off of the top of my desk, still feeling pretty groggy, I looked over at the clock on the wall and I seen that it was six o'clock. Texas was still setting in the same chair, but he had it kicked back and had it leaning up against the wall, and he looked to be sound asleep. I didn't see no sign of the Dutchman.

"Texas," I roared, and he kind of jumped and woke up, dropping the chair down on its all four legs.

"What? What is it?" he said, pulling out his six-shooter and looking around the room kind of wild-like.

"Put that goddamn thing away," I said. "Ain't nobody here but just the two of us. Where the hell's the Dutchman?"

"Oh," Texas said, holstering his revolver and setting back down. "He pulled out of here last night, just right after you passed out."

"I never passed out," I said. "I just went to sleep for a while, that's all. A man's got to get his sleep, ain't he? Right before a big battle, ain't a man got to get his sleep? What the hell you let him go for?"

"Who?" said Texas, a stupid look on his face.

"The damn Dutchman," I said. "Who else?"

"Oh. Well, what else could I do?" he said. "What the hell you let old Scratchy go for?"

"Goddamn it," I said. There was still a little whiskey in my glass, and I picked it up and finished it off. "So the Dutchman run out on me too, did he? Well then, it's just me and you, Texas. Just me and you."

"And four of them Bensons a-coming," he said.

"That's right," I said. "Little Red and them other three."

"What's their names, anyway?" he asked me. "I been trying to recall."

"I don't know their goddamned names," I snapped at him. "Who gives a damn about their names anyhow?"

"Let's see, now," he said, just ignoring what I said and scratching his head real thoughtful. Obviously, he give a damn. "Seems to me like they was Loren and Orren and something or other different, like—Elmo, maybe. Yeah. That's it. It'll be Little Red, Loren, Orren and Elmo. That's who it'll be coming to town. High noon."

"Shut up," I said. "There's four of them, and that's all I give a damn about."

"Barjack?" he said, kind of like a question.

"What?" I grumbled back at him.

"You got a plan?" he asked me.

"A plan?" I said. My head still wasn't clear from the night before.

"What the hell are we going to do, Barjack?" he said. "When them four shows up, what're we going to do?"

I stood up, scratching my head and pacing the floor. "Hell, I don't know," I said. "I got to think on it some. Right now I just don't know. We're going to do something, though. I don't aim to just let them assholes kill me."

I kind of slapped at my coat pockets like I was hunting for something, but I didn't rightly know what it was I was hunting. All I come up with was just a cigar. I poked it in my mouth and found a match and lit the damn thing. I didn't really want it just then, but I wanted something what I couldn't quite figure it out.

"Barjack," Texas said. "I been thinking."

"Huh. That's something new for you be taking up, ain't it?" I said.

"I been thinking that maybe old Scratchy was right," he said. "It looks to me like there's only one thing to do. You got to get out of town."

I turned on him real fast. "I can't do that," I said, and I like to have bit off the end of my cigar. "You better give up on thinking, Texas. Leave that part of it to me."

"Hell, Barjack," he said, "it's the only way. All right, you think about it, then. We can't do this thing. You and me fight them four? We can't do it. Not just the two of us. Not and live to tell about it, we can't."

"I got a new wife here," I said. "I can't just turn tail and run off."

"You won't do her no good dead," Texas said. "And besides, she's—Listen. You can leave town for just a while. That's all. Just long enough to let this thing blow over. Then come on back after that if you want to. Your business and all will still be here waiting for you. What you got to lose? You ain't got nothing to lose playing it like that."

Well, I thought it over. I really did. And it did kind of make sense, but then I asked myself, Was Texas right in saying that I didn't have nothing to lose? Would old Peester really hold my job open for me? I made most of my living out of Harvey's Hooch House, but it was my marshaling job that allowed me to keep out any competition, and the town council paid my deputies too, and that was how I kept order in the Hooch House. If I was to lose my marshaling job, things could start to fall apart for me there in Asininity. And I had a little feeling gnawing at a corner of my brain a-telling me that Peester and the rest of the town council just might welcome a chance to get rid of me without having to just to come right out and fire me to my face.

They was happy enough to get me ten years ago, but for

nine and half of them years now things had been right peaceful. I had got the feeling more than once that there was elements in town that felt like they didn't really need no tough-ass, town-taming marshal no more. This Benson business was the only real trouble that had hit town in a long time, and it wouldn't be hitting at all if I was out of the way.

Then, too, I wondered, if I was to run off for a spell the way they was wanting me to, would my lovely Lillian still be setting there in my little new house just a-waiting patiently for me to come back? And what about the Hooch House? Old Bonnie would likely rob me blind while I was off skulking around. I wouldn't be able to make the payments on all my various properties, and old Peester would wind up owning it all. Anyhow, them all seemed to be possibilities. They was most certain real good questions, and I couldn't answer none of them for sure one way or the other, and without I could do that in a satisfactory way, I couldn't hardly afford to leave town, not even for a while. Thinking it over like that, I come to see that my holdings was all kind of precarious without me setting right there and holding on tight to the reins. So that was that.

"I just can't do her," I said. "I got to stay here and face up to my duty, Texas. I got to. I done some ornery things in my day, but I never shirked on my duty."

Well, old Texas really surprised the hell out of me just then. He showed some gumption, which was a side of himself that I had never seen before. He just come right across the room without no warning and laid a hand on my shoulder and spun me around to face him, and then he grabbed ahold of me by my shirtfront. He was gritting his teeth, and his face was damn near touching mine. I could feel his hot stinky whiskey breath on my face.

"Damn it, Barjack," he said, "you got to get out. I'll go on over to the stable and saddle up your horse myself. I'll even saddle up an extra horse, so you can take it along and make better time by switching off. Don't say nothing to nobody. Just mount up and go. I'll think of something to tell old Peester for you and some way to explain things to your wife. Come on. Let's go to the stable."

He started to pull me toward the door, and whenever I resisted by pulling back, he turned of a sudden and bashed me right up along the side of the head. Damn, I never knowed old Texas could hit that hard. I fell heavy into the wall. He reached for my lapel again. "Come on, you old fart," he said. That made me mad. I figured at the most I was middle-aged. I swung a right and caught him on the jaw. He staggered back a few steps, stopped, shook his head, and then looked up at me.

"That the way you want it?" he said.

"Come on, you little runt," I said.

I stepped away from the wall and put up my dukes the way a real prizefighter does and made ready to have it out with old Texas, but the sly little son of a bitch ducked his head low and run smack into my belly, wrapping his arms around my waist and carrying me backward into the desk. The bottle and the glasses there kind of rocked, but they didn't fall. Then the both of us fell over to the side and crashed down onto the floor. He still had that bear hug on me, and I commenced to pounding him about the head and shoulders, but I don't think I was hurting him none. He had drawed his head down into his shoulders kind of like a turtle, and so I didn't have much of a target.

I struggled up to my feet, dragging him along with me, and then I raised up my knee. I meant to get his balls with it, but I missed and only rammed my knee into his midsection. He let out all his air with a poof, turned me loose, and backed away.

"You little turncoat bastard," I said, and I was puffing. I was getting too old and soft for this kind of activity. I knowed that. I also knowed that I was still tough enough and mean enough to whip that snot-nosed kid one way or another. But I sure didn't have it in me the way I used to have. It might seem funny, but just at that moment I thought about my wedding night again and my pitiful showing there. No, sirree, I didn't have what I used to have.

"I'm just trying to do what's best for you," Texas said. "That's all."

"Hell," I said, "you little runt. Why don't you just go ahead and run off the way all the others has done. I don't need them, and I don't need you, neither." Well, that, of course, was a monstrous big lie, but I just wanted to say it anyway. I knowed he was lying to me. He wasn't just only thinking about what was good for me. There had to be something else. Maybe he was scared to death of fighting the Bensons with me and just didn't want to own up to it. The only way he could figure to get out of it was if I was to run off. Then there wouldn't be no fight, and he'd be safe and wouldn't have to own up to being chicken. That was the best I could come up with.

"I ain't going," he said. "You're the one that's going."

I stepped toward him and made a fake with my right, and when he went to block it, I popped him upside the jaw with a left hook. Blood run down from out the corner of his mouth. He spit on the floor. Then he raised up his fists and took on a right serious look.

"Old man," he said, "I'm fixing to whip your ass."

He come at me a-jabbing his left fist into my face, and I blocked most of them, but he caught me a time or two, and it did sting. I think he bloodied my nose. I backed up all the while, but then of a sudden I ducked low, and I drove a right fist real hard into his gut. He whoofed again, and I moved in quick. I got my head right down against his shoulder, and his arms was just a-flailing useless over my shoulders and flapping on my back, while I was pounding his kidneys as hard as I could with both fists.

He took it pretty good, though. I got to give him that. Then, when he seen his chance, he slapped me aside of the head, right on top of my ear, and I thought for sure that he had busted my eardrum. He might have, too. Goddamn, I commenced to hearing the loudest ringing in my head I had ever heard before, and it kind of made me dizzy. I still hear it sometimes. I staggered back away from him. He didn't come after me, though. He stood there panting, trying to get back his breath from the pounding I had just give him. I shook my head, trying to clear it of the damn ringing.

By and by, Texas straightened up some and raised his

fists again and started in moving at me. I held up my open palms. "Hold on, now, Texas," I said. "Wait. Wait just a minute."

"Had enough, old man?" he asked me.

"No," I said. "Hell no. I'm fixing to stomp your ass good, but just wait a minute, will you?"

He stood still with a real curious look on his face, and I turned around and picked up the whiskey bottle. I poured a short drink into my glass. Then I looked back at Texas, holding up the bottle. "You want some?" I asked him.

He dropped his guard and walked toward me. "Why not?" he said. Just as old Texas stepped up close to the desk and reached out for his glass which was setting there, I bashed him on the back of the head as hard as I could with that whiskey bottle. Pieces of glass went every which way, and whiskey splashed all over everything, and old Texas just kind of slumped over on the desk. He was out cold, and blood was running through his hair and down his neck and puddling a little on my desktop. I kind of hoped I hadn't killed him, but I had more things than that to worry about just then. I glanced at the clock and seen that it was going on toward seven. I had just a little over five hours to figure out how I was going to handle them Bensons when they come riding in.

I pulled Texas's gunbelt off of him, and then I dragged his limp body into the nearest cell and shut and locked the door. I had enough to deal with, and I sure didn't want him coming back to his senses and playing hell with me no more that morning. I went back in my back room and splashed some water on my face to kind of clear my head, and I recalled how stinky old Texas's breath had been, so I rinsed my mouth out some, too. I sure did need some more cleaning up, but it would just have to wait some. I went back out to my desk and set down. There was that list me and Texas had wrote up. I looked at it. Every one of them bastards had bailed out on me. Well, old Gap Tooth hadn't had much choice in the matter, but he was just as gone as the rest of them was. I wadded the list up and threw it on the floor. Who else? I asked myself. Who else can I get?

Chapter Eighteen

I strapped on my old faithful Merwin and Hulbert Company self-extracting forty-five-caliber revolver and another six-shooter, a damned old Colt, tucked two more into my belt, and picked up a shotgun. I checked them all to make sure they was all loaded to full capacity, and then I left the office. I didn't worry none about them gun barrels poking into my thighs, neither. It was seven o'clock in the morning. I walked over to the law office of old Randall Peester. He was just unlocking his front door when I got there.

"Barjack," he said, like he was surprised to see me, and I reckoned that he was. No one in Asininity had seen me out and about for years at such an ungodly early hour as what it was then. "What can I do for you?"

"You can arm yourself," I said, following him on into the office, "and get ready to stand up against them Bensons with me when they get here. I can't face them bastards all by my lonesome."

"What happened to your posse?" he asked me. "Didn't I authorize a posse, and haven't I been paying extra deputies?" I was afraid that he was going to bring that up, and

I really didn't have time to explain all the details about how I had lost all them boys.

"The assholes has all deserted me," I said.

"Your regular deputies?" he asked.

"Them too," I said. "Well? What about it?"

Peester walked on into the inner office, which was his private office, and moved around behind his big desk. I followed him all the way in and stood facing him across the desk.

"I'll have to stop all that deputy pay that's been going to your office," he said. "That's what."

"No, I mean what about getting your guns?" I said.

"I don't even own a gun, Barjack," the son of a bitch said, but I knowed he was lying to me through his yellow teeth. "You'll have to look somewhere else."

"I got plenty of damn guns," I said. "That ain't no problem. Come on with me."

"I'm no gunfighter, Barjack," he said.

"You can shoot a rifle, can't you?" I said. "Or a shotgun? Hell, anyone can shoot a shotgun. All you have to do with it is to just point it. You can't miss with a shotgun. Here. You can take this one right here. It's loaded and ready to go."

"I'm sorry, Barjack," he said, folding his hands in his lap like a sissy. "I just can't do it. I've never fired a gun in anger or at another human being in all my life. My whole life has been devoted to the study of the law. You'll just have to find someone else."

"There ain't no one else," I said. "I had them all, and they've all done quit on me."

"Then the only thing I can think of," he said, "is for you to get yourself safely out of town."

"You too? All of a damn sudden, everyone wants me to get out of town. Well, hell, sure damn. I get it now. You'd like it just fine if I was to leave, wouldn't you?" I said. "Then you could just go right on ahead and foreclose on all my goddamn property."

"Now, Barjack," he said, "I resent that implication. I assure you, I'm just thinking of what's good for you. That's all. Get out of town. Lay low for a while. The Bensons will leave when they discover that you're not here."

"It seems like everyone just to wants to get me the hell out of town," I said. "Well, I ain't going."

"Then I can't help you," he said, "not unless you want my help in drawing up your last will and testament."

Well, I didn't bother answering that smart-ass remark. Instead I just stormed out of there and slammed his door behind me. I walked straight on over to the Hooch House, where I found old Aubrey cleaning up the bar, getting ready for another business day just like there wasn't nothing wrong at all. I was glad that Bonnie wasn't nowhere to be seen, but I figured that she was still sacked out upstairs. Hell, she was worse than me. She never had been knowed to get her fat ass out of bed before at least ten o'clock, not after the late hours she always kept in the Hooch House. Aubrey looked up when I come in, looking real surprised to see me. Harrison Dingle was setting there a-writing in his notebook, and he looked up like he was real pleased to see me come in. I didn't have no time to worry about his ass, though. I went straight over to the bar.

"Good morning, Barjack," Aubrey said. "Cup of coffee?"

"Aubrey, old partner," I said. "Get that old scattergun out. I need you."

"What for?" he said, his eyes popping wide.

"It's the fifteenth, Aubrey, the fifteenth, goddamn it," I said. "Look at your calendar. It's here. It's on us. They'll be in town at high noon. The Bensons. The Bensons is coming. We got to be ready for them, boy. Come on."

"I—I can't do that, Barjack," Aubrey said. "Why, I'd be shaking so bad I wouldn't even be able to point the thing. Anyhow, I'm not a deputy. I'm a bartender. That's all. I ain't paid to fight, and I sure ain't paid to get shot at."

"Aubrey," I said, "either you pick up that goddamned shotgun out from under that bar and come along with me, or you can just start in hunting yourself up another job in some other town."

Well, old Aubrey really braced up at that. He swelled up his chest, as much as he could, stuck his chin out at me, and he said, "Well, we'll just see what Miss Bonnie has to say about that."

"Goddamn you, Aubrey," I said, "and goddamn Bonnie Boodle and her fat ass, too. I own more of this here place than what she does, and if I say you're fired, then by God you're fired. Take off that damned apron what belongs to me and get the hell out of here."

Just then old Bonnie commenced to flouncing down the stairs. I heard her tromping noise, and I looked around to see who it was a-coming. I had a fearful premonition, though, but I swear to God, I had never seen her even awake that early in the day before, much less up and out of bed, not in all the years I had knowed her. It was like some kind of miracle, only it was coming from the wrong source to be one of them. It was like a miracle, but only it was coming straight from the bowels of hell.

"Don't you be goddamning me and my ass, Barjack, you double-dealing, back-stabbing son of a bitch," she shrieked. "You ain't got nothing to do with my ass nomore." She was coming down the steps fast, her tits just a-bouncing. They looked to me like if she wasn't careful they might just get slung clear loose of her chest and fly across the room. I bucked up and turned to face her.

"Bonnie," I said, "I knocked you out once, and I'll do it again if I have to. You get on back to bed."

"You keep your mouth shut about my bed," she snarled. "You ain't got no business with my bed no more neither."

By that time she was all the way down the stairs, and she was moving fast around behind the bar with her flesh a-bouncing all over the place. I felt some relieved, 'cause she wasn't headed in my direction. I figured she was just only going around there to stand beside old Aubrey and defend his rights against me, and I was prepared to stand my ground as the major owner of the place. Well, I figured wrong. She come up real quick with that scattergun I had told Aubrey to get, and she swung it up over the bar and pointed it in a real unfriendly way right over into my general vicinity.

"Bonnie," I said, holding up a hand, and she thumbed

160

back a hammer. "Now, Bonnie." She thumbed back the second hammer. "Don't do that, Bonnie." She raised that damn gun up to her shoulder, and I took out a-running just as hard as I could go. When I come within two or three paces of the front door, I just took a headlong dive and crashed right through it, and right behind me I heard that damn gun go off. I hit the street headfirst and plowed dirt with my nose, but I didn't catch no buckshot in my behind, so I felt lucky.

I knowed, though, that there was another barrel on that gun with another trigger and hammer, and I also knowed that Bonnie had thumbed back both hammers. I got back to my feet just as fast as I could and went running for the other side of the street. Sure enough, Bonnie got herself to the door and took another shot at me. Blooie! It was a damn good thing for me I had got way over across the street. She missed again. Her gun was empty then, and I hadn't been hit. I felt a little bolder because of that, and so I stepped right out into the middle of the street and I shook my fist at her right menacing-like to show her just how displeased I was.

"You could have killed me, goddamn you," I yelled across at the wild angry bitch. "If you're so damned anxious to go shooting at folks, you ought to just load that gun back up and wait on the Bensons to get in here and help me out."

"I hope they blow your goddamn brains all over the street," she screamed, and I reckon the whole damn town could hear what she was saying. "Only thing is," she went on, "you ain't got none. I hope they blow your damn balls off instead. See how your new wife likes you then. With no balls."

I was about to yell at her again and return the latest insult right back to her, when I noticed my own loaded double-barreled shotgun laying there in the street where I had dropped it when I crashed, and I noticed, too, that Bonnie had laid her eyes on it at just about the same time. And she was considerable closer to it than I was. Well, she run right out to it and grabbed it up, and I took out fast for the nearest little space between two buildings. I heard that gun roar behind me, and I heard a window glass shatter. I ducked in between the buildings just as the second barrel fired, and that time I felt some splinters or something stinging against my back and neck, but I made it most to safety, and I knowed for sure then that she didn't have nothing left to shoot at me with.

I sudden felt a kind of roiling in my guts, and I hurried down to the far end of the lane which I had escaped into. Then I doubled over with a hell of a pain deep down in my innards, and I commenced to puking my guts out. Oh Lord, it was awful. I figure it was caused by all the worrying over the Bensons and the getting shot at and the pounding I had took from Texas and all. Maybe all the whiskey I had drunk had something to do with it too, but I don't really think so. It was good whiskey. I never did drink none of that cheap stuff.

At last I quit puking, but when I straightened myself up, I could see that I had made a bit of a mess of my shirtfront, and my mouth sure tasted nasty, so I decided to skulk my way back to my office where I could go into the back room and clean up just a little. I didn't want to get myself killed in that untidy condition. I managed to get over to the office without no one seeing me but just old Gimpy Hotchkins's snot-nosed kid, and I sure didn't give a damn what he seen or thought. I always did believe he was some kind of a half-wit anyhow. Texas was still out cold when I walked past the cell, but I figured he was probably alive. I decided that if I lived into the afternoon, I'd check up on him. I went on into the back room and took off my nasty clothes. I washed myself up a little, rinsed out my mouth to get rid of the taste, and put on clean clothes. Then I went back out to my desk to set and think for a while. I sure needed to find myself some help.

Well, the only name that come into my mind was that of old Hardass Taylor. He didn't like me none, and I was plenty mad at old Hardass 'cause of the way he had took them four cowboy deputies away from me, and the way he had talked to me on that occasion too, but at last I decided that under the special circumstances I was facing, I had ought to swaller my pride and go see him. If I was to tell him that it was a life-and-death matter, that them Bensons was coming right into town to kill me, and if I was to remind him that they was low-down cattle rustlers in the first place, well, he might just give in and bring his entire damned crew into town and take care of the whole problem for me.

I figured that I would just about have time to ride on out there to the Taylor spread and bring Hardass and his boys back to town by high noon. I hoped that he wouldn't put up too much argument with me before giving in, 'cause I sure didn't have the time to waste that way. But I did feel better having made that big decision to go to Hardass for some help. That seemed like the answer. It had to be, I thought, 'cause there just wasn't no other way I could see. I jumped up right then and damn near run all the way down to the stable to get my horse. Old Porkbarrel was just lounging around there, and I told him to hurry his ass up and get my critter saddled for me.

"You leaving town, Barjack?" he asked me.

I felt like hitting him in the mouth, but if I done that, he wouldn't have got my horse saddled for me. "No, I ain't," I said. "Well, yes, I am, but I'll be back before high noon. Hurry up with that damned saddle."

Porkbarrel finally got my nag saddled, and I mounted up and rode hard and fast out of town. I knowed that Porkbarrel and anyone else who seen me going would think that I was running away the way so many of them wanted me to do, but I didn't give a damn just then what they was thinking. I'd be back soon enough with my reinforcements, and I'd show them all then. I wasn't for sure, but I thought that I could ride that horse hard all the way out to Hardass's place and back without killing him, and anyhow I knowed that I had to try.

Well, I got to the ranch all right after a good hard ride, and I was panting and sweating, but not nearly like what that poor horse was doing. When I started to ride through the big gate to go up to the ranch house, I was stopped there by Chicago and Shorty Joe.

"Sorry, Barjack," Chicago said. "The boss said he don't want you poking around out here."

"I come out on official business, boys," I said. "Where is old Hardass?"

"He's up at the ranch house," Shorty Joe said, "but he don't want to see you. It's like Chicago said."

"Move on out of the road," I said.

"Barjack," Shorty said, "old Hardass said if we seen you trying to come onto his property, we was to shoot you dead."

I give them two cowboys my hardest look just then. "Are you two fixing to gun down a law officer?" I said. " 'Cause if you do, they'll hang you for sure. That is, if I don't get you first. I know I can get one of you. Which one would rather get shot and which one would rather hang? I'll do my best to accommodate you boys."

"Barjack," Chicago said, "we don't want to fight you. We're just telling you what old Hardass said, that's all."

"All right, you told me," I said. "Now get out of my way."

The boys moved aside, and I rode on down the lane to the big ranch house, and sure enough, I found old Hardass right there a-waiting. He had come out on the porch to see who it was that had pounded hoofs up there so hard. I hauled in on the reins, and my old horse was panting and blowing and slobbering.

"Barjack," he said when he seen me, "you no-good bastard, what are you trying to do? Kill that horse?"

"It's him or me," I said. "Round up your boys and follow me back to town. There ain't no time to waste."

"What the hell are you talking about?" Hardass said.

"The Bensons is coming," I said. "They're due to hit town at high noon."

"That ain't my problem," he said.

"Listen here, Hardass," I said. "There's four of them, and they're planning to do murder on me. It's your civic duty to assist the law in a case like this."

"Don't try to pull that on me, Barjack," he said. "You wouldn't have got them four boys from my crew in the first damn place if I'd been here when Texas Jack come around to get them. Well, I'm here now, and you can just turn around and ride on back to town."

"Them Bensons are like to kill me," I said with some degree of desperation in my voice.

"Far as I can tell," Hardass said, "they'll be doing us all a favor. Now, get the hell off my property."

"Them's hard words, Hardass," I told him. "Hard and cold."

"They express my heartfelt sentiments, Barjack," the bastard said.

"Wait just a minute, now," I said. "It's one thing if you want to see me get killed. I ain't going to let that hurt my feelings none. But them Bensons is notorious rustlers. Have you forgot that? If they get away with killing me and getting rid of the only law around here just like that, what's to stop them from running off every head of beef you got out here? Think about that. Have you thought about that?"

"I've thought about it," Hardass said. "I believe I'll be better off with all my boys out here watching the herd than if I was to let them go back to town with you. Now, get out of here before I have you shot."

Chapter Nineteen

The ride on back into town that time seemed to me to be a hell of a lot longer than the ride out had been, and then for sure I really didn't want to kill my damn horse along the way. As it was, he stumbled a time or two and damn near went down with me on his back. I kept him going, though. I had to get back before high noon. I didn't want to ride into town, or come limping in afoot, after the Bensons had done arrived and not know where they might be lurking. I had planned all along to be ready for them, even to have myself an ambush laid, and now if I didn't hurry my ass on back in, they could be the ones doing the ambushing on me. I surely couldn't allow them to do that. Well, I made it back, and I didn't kill the horse, but he wasn't feeling too chipper, neither, when I dropped him off at Porkbarrel's place. I took note of the time and seen that it was nine-thirty. I had me just two and a half hours left to—I damn near said "left to live."

Well, I hustled on back to my office, and you can imagine my surprise when I opened the door and seen Texas Jack setting there in my own chair right behind my own desk with Lillian, my own wife, a-setting on his lap and smooching with him. They heard the door open and me stomp in, and Texas jumped up faster than Lillian did, so he dumped her right down on the floor. She scrambled up to her feet and smoothed her dress. Their both faces was red, as well they should have been with what they was up to. My own face must have turned red with rage, for I was sudden primed to kill.

"Barjack," said Texas, "this ain't what you think it is."

"What I just seen," I said, "I seen pretty clear. Don't seem to me that thinking's got nothing to do with it."

"Lillian—uh—Miz Barjack just come down here looking for you," Texas said, "and she seen me locked up in that cell. I told her that I'd got locked in there by accident, and she got the keys and let me out."

"Then I saw how his face was beat up," Lillian said, "and I was just—"

"I know what you was just," I said, interrupting her and keeping her from making up some lame and lying excuse for her shameful behavior. "I seen it. You get yourself on back over to the house and wait for me there. I'll deal with you later." If I'm still alive, I added in my thoughts.

"What are you going to do?" she said.

"Never you trouble your pretty head with that little question," I said. "I had ought to kill the both of you right now. That's what I ought to do, and wouldn't no man alive blame me none for it, but I ain't decided on it just yet. Now, you get on home."

Lillian left the office, scurrying past me to get out of the door, and Texas was standing tense there behind my desk like he was ready to go for his gun if I was to go for mine. Well, he didn't know it, but he didn't really have to worry none about that. I had never in my whole life drawed a gun on a man face-to-face. I always figured that was just a damn stupid thing to do, not knowing how fast either party could get his shooter out or how straight he could shoot when he was in that kind of a hurry. Just as soon as Lillian was well on down the street, I put a real long look on my hard old face.

"I can't hardly believe what you just done to me, Texas," I said. "Me, what brung you into the law-enforcement business and taught you everything I knowed. Me, who trusted you right up until the end when you quit on me in my time of need. Then, as if you hadn't hurt me bad enough already, you went and took up with my own newly married wife while I was out of town on the business of life and death— my own life and death. I trusted you, Texas. You was like a son to me, or at least maybe a little brother. Hell, I left my own family when I was just only thirteen years old and never seen none of them again. You was all the family I had, boy. I sure as hell ought to kill you, but I—"

"Barjack," he said, "she's a whore."

"Goddamn you," I said. "What you done was bad enough without you go calling my Lillian names."

"I ain't calling names, Barjack," he said. "Before she come out here, she was one of them what you call high-class prostitutes back in Saint Looey or someplace. It was old Dick Custer told me that. Well, he didn't tell me to my face. He told Chicago and Remuda, and it was them told me what he said. They told me at breakfast the next morning. They said that she'd been run out of near every town she'd been in before, and she was looking for some place to light. She must have figured marrying up with you would set her up right well. That's what they said that old Custer said. I wasn't going to say nothing to you about it, but now that you're thinking about killing me, I reckon that maybe I ought to. Ought to tell you, that is."

"Dick Custer said all that?" I asked him. "Old Dick Custer?" And I was recalling them looks that old Custer had got on his face, the first one when I first mentioned her name to him, and the second when he had looked her in the face that time and give her his congratulations on our wedding. Them looks had made me suspicious, but I had chose not to think about them no more. Well, I turned toward the wall and leaned my left arm up against it and laid my face on my forearm like I was crying at the sad news I had just got.

"Barjack," Texas said, and his voice was just chock-full

of pity, "I'm real sorry. Hell, I didn't want to be the one
to give you that terrible news, but it ain't the worst thing
in the world. Why, you took up with old Bonnie for a long
time. And I wouldn't never have done what I done, but she
started it. She was saying how you couldn't get it up the
other night, and—"

Well, that done it. I just couldn't let the little son of a
bitch live any longer, knowing that he knowed that about
me. I still had my face laying on my arm and my back
turned to Texas, but I had them extra two revolvers stuck
in my belt, so I just slipped one of them out in front of me,
and he never seen what I was doing. He never even sus-
pected it. Still holding the six-gun between my belly and
the wall, I cocked it real easy, and then I turned of a sudden
and pointed it right at old Texas, right at his chest. He
yelled and dropped to the floor behind the desk just as I
pulled the trigger, and my slug slammed useless into the
wall just behind where he had been standing.

As I was thumbing back the hammer for another shot,
Texas popped up behind the desk with his shooter out, and
he fired a shot that tore a tiny piece of my right ear off. I
don't know if you know it or not, but ears bleed like hell
when they're tore, and the blood was running free down
my neck. I yelled real loud and sent another slug at him,
but he dropped out of sight again just as soon as he had
made his own shot. I missed the son of a bitch again. I
ducked through the door real quick-like and pressed myself
against the outside wall. Slowly I peered around the edge
of the open doorway, and as I was doing that, Texas was
just as slow in peeping up over the top of the desk.

We seen each other at the same time, and we each pulled
our triggers at the same time. Like before, neither one of
us hit his mark. And we both ducked back behind our cover
at almost the same time. Damn it, I wanted to kill old Texas
just then, but I couldn't figure how the hell to get the job
done. I should have got him with my first shot, and I cussed
myself real good for having missed that one. Now here I
was in what amounted almost to a fair fight. And with my

own damn deputy. Well, former deputy. I felt like a damned fool.

"Texas," I called out. It was real quiet. "Texas. Can you hear me?"

" 'Course I can hear you," he said. "You're just over there by the door."

"Well, listen to me, then," I said. "Don't shoot no more."

"I won't if you won't," he said.

"I shot first without thinking," I said. "It was what you said about my wife made me do it. Let's call this thing off. You and me been friends too long to go killing each other."

"Well, okay," he said.

I peeked around through the doorway then, and he was standing up and holstering his six-gun. I raised mine up real quick and shot him in the chest. A red splotch appeared there where I hit him, and he just looked kind of surprised at first. He tilted his head down a little in order to take a look at the hole in his chest, then he kind of relaxed and he just fell back into my chair and set there dead. He looked almost natural setting there like that. He'd have looked total natural if I'd have propped his feet up for him. I felt bad a little about killing old Texas that way, but I just couldn't stand the thought of him or any other man being alive and knowing the awful truth about my wedding night. Then something made me think that if Lillian had told Texas, she just might tell someone else. Well, I really didn't want to have to kill her too, but I knowed I'd sure have to do something about it. I just didn't have the time for it right then.

I went around behind my desk and shoved old Texas out of my chair for the last time. Then I set down to reload my revolver I had been shooting and to think for a while. It wasn't long before old Peester showed his face in my office door, and damned if that schoolteaching Dingle bastard wasn't right behind him. When they seen me just setting there real calm, they figured everything was all right, and they stepped on in. Dingle kept kind of behind old Peester, though.

"Howdy, Peester," I said. "What the hell is that you got stuck onto your backside?"

"What?" he said. "Oh. It's Harrison Dingle, of course. You know Harrison."

"What's he doing in here?" I asked.

"He's just an interested citizen," said Peester.

"What you interested in, schoolteacher?" I said, but Peester kept him from answering my question.

"Barjack," he said, "what was all that shooting? Was it the Bensons?"

"They ain't due till high noon," I said, and I pointed to old Texas where he was laying. Peester, with Dingle glued right on his ass, stepped on in farther and looked around the desk to see what I was showing him. He stiffened up and his eyes went big and round, and I'll be damned if Dingle didn't flip open his shittin' notebook and start in to writing.

"That's Texas Jack," Peester said.

"I don't believe he was really from Texas," I said. "I think the little lying son of a bitch really come from Iowa or some damn place like that. Likely come off a farm. Maybe Indiana. Illinois maybe. I don't think he ever even seen Texas."

"But that's Texas Jack Dooly," Peester said, his mouth hanging open. "Your deputy. Who—What—"

"I had to kill the little bastard," I said. "He tried to beat the crap out of me early this morning, so I throwed him in a cell for assaulting an officer. When I come in here just a little while ago, he had got out somehow, and he commenced to shooting at me. I didn't have no choice, Peester. I done what I had to do."

"But Texas Jack—"

"Peester," I said, "do you reckon you could grab someone out there on the street on your way back to your office and have them do something about this?" I nodded toward the stiff on the floor, and Peester stammered a little and kind of nodded and turned and walked out of the office shaking his head. Dingle walked right behind him, still writing as he walked, and looking back over his shoulder at me or the stiff two or three times on his way. He run into the door frame and had to take another run at it to get out.

Well, that was that. My guns was all loaded full again, and I had to plan for the Bensons. I was all alone in this deal, and I didn't like that. I thought about the advice most everyone had give me, to just up and run, and my mind went back to that time in Manhattan when I was just thirteen years old or so, and I had kicked the ass of that Irish kid. I had knowed that the Five Point bastards would be coming after me, and I had ran like hell to save my life. It had seemed like the only intelligent thing to do at the time.

Even so, I didn't want to do that this time, and it didn't have nothing to do with no kind of false pride. Hell, I'll run and hide to save my ass anytime. But whenever I run off from old Manhattan all them years ago, I didn't have nothing back there to lose. In Asininity I had everything. Well, almost everything. I sure as hell didn't have the wife I thought I had. I still had me a wife, though, and she was still just as great to look at as ever. Couldn't nothing take that away from her. But she wasn't the lady I had thought she was. She was just another whore—a high-class whore, but a whore all the same. I still had all my property, though, and I still had my job and my business. Hell, I practical run Asininity. I didn't want to give all that up.

But I got to thinking about Lillian then. I got to thinking about how much I had been took with all her loveliness and charm and all, and then I recalled the terrible events of our wedding night and the scene later with her and old Texas. But the worst thing I could recall was that she had actual told Texas about my shame. I looked at the clock on the wall. My time was getting short, but I couldn't help myself. I had to go and have a talk with Lillian.

Chapter Twenty

Some son of a bitch, I don't remember who it was, once told me that I could have easy walked the distance from my office to my new house in less time than what it takes to go to the stable and saddle up my horse and ride over there. Well, I don't know if that's true or not, but even though I didn't have much time left for myself before the big showdown at high noon, maybe I didn't have much time left to be alive on this earth, and even though I was real anxious to have that little talk with my newly acquired and even more recently spoiled wife, I went on down to the stable to get old Porkbarrel to saddle up my old nag.

The poor thing was still wheezing some from the recent hard riding I had give him out to old Hardass Taylor's place and back, but I went on and rode him easy on over to the house, and I hitched him there to that cute little white picket fence. The very sight of that place and the thought of what it had almost been for me like to brought a tear to my eye, but it never quite done that. I walked right through the gate and stomped up to the front porch. Then, without bothering to knock or nothing, I just barged right through and on into the living room. After all, it was my goddamned house, and that was my goddamned wife in there, even though I had failed to do anything to her about it thus far.

She was just setting there on that damned love seat thing, looking like there wasn't nothing wrong about anything she ever done in her whole sweet and innocent life. She smiled at me and stood up and walked over toward me, but I held out my hands to keep her away. I kind of knowed that if she was to put them lovely arms around my neck I wouldn't be able to say the kinds of things I wanted to say, and I didn't want her to think that I was that easy to deal with and to make a sucker out of. But then all of a sudden, standing there and looking at her like that, I just couldn't seem to find them all-important words. My head was chock-full of stuff to say to her, but my double-crossing tongue wouldn't cooperate with my damn dull brain. So she wound up being the first one to start in talking.

"Barjack, darling," she said, and oh, her voice was sweet, but I tried my best to steel myself to it. "I know just what you must be thinking about me right now. But before you say anything you'll regret, let me explain things to you."

"Goddamn it," I said, but she shooshed me up and kept right on a-talking.

"Wait a minute," she said. "Let me finish. Then you can say anything you want to say to me. I went over to your office looking for you. I was worried sick about you. I still am. I wanted to find out if there was anything I could do to help. You might be surprised, but I can handle a rifle. I got over there and found Texas Jack in the cell, locked up. He told me that he had locked himself in the cell by accident. What was I to do? I believed him, of course. He was your deputy."

"He wasn't no more," I said. "He up and quit on me, and then he pounded up on me too, so I locked him in there my own self. He was a prisoner in there. You let my prisoner out of jail."

"I had no way of knowing that," she said. "He didn't tell me."

"He said you was a high-class whore," I blurted out of

a sudden, and then it got real quiet. Well, I had let it out. The both of us just kind of stood there silent, me looking down at the floor. I don't know where she was looking. Finally she broke up that heavy silence with her sweet voice.

"And you believed him?" she said. "Without even asking me about it?"

"I wouldn't have," I said. "I'd have called him a damn liar and shot him dead, but only he said that it was old Dick Custer what told it on you, and then I had done seen you a-setting on Texas and doing . . . what you was doing."

"Barjack," she said, "I never lied to you. Did you ever ask me about my past?"

"Well, no," I said. "I never, but I—"

"Then I don't see what you have to complain about," she said. "If you're so concerned about what my life was like before we met, you should have asked me about it before you asked me to marry you. But you didn't. Did you?"

With them last few words, she had moved right up to me and put her hands on my shoulders, and she was looking up into my face with them great big eyes of hers, and I was melting fast. I felt like somehow I had let her get the best of me, and I didn't want to let that happen, so I looked away real quick, and I reached up and took hold of her wrists and took her hands off of me.

"Lillian," I said, "I seen you setting on old Texas and smooching with him. I seen that with my own eyes, and that ain't got nothing to do with your past. That was well after you become my wife."

She turned away from me then and hung her head. "He told me that he knew about me," she said. "He said he'd heard it from Sheriff Custer yesterday, just like he told you. Then he threatened to tell you about it if I didn't—Well, you know."

"Why, that dirty little son of a bitch," I said. "Goddamn it, if I hadn't already gone and killed him, I'd go right back over there and do it again. He threatened you? He did that? That goddamned little bastard."

"It's not that I wanted to hide my past from you, darling," she said. "I just didn't want you to have to hear about it from someone else. And now that's happened anyway. You have heard it from someone else, so it was all for nothing, and now you hate me. Well, I won't hold you to your promise, Barjack. If you want a divorce, I won't stand in your way."

And I'll be goddamned all the way straight into hell's deepest pits and hottest flames if she didn't start in to crying and sobbing and daubing at her eyes. Well, that got to me. Even if she was a whore, she was still the most loveliest creature I had ever laid my eyes on, and in spite of everything that had just happened, I guess I was still real hard smit with her. I couldn't hardly stand seeing her like that. I rushed on over to her and put my arms around her and held her close. I could feel her trembling all over with her sobs, and I didn't want to do nothing then but just only comfort her. I swear I forgot all about the ugly things I had seen and the nasty words that Texas had said and the coming possible end of my life and those goddamned Bensons and everything else except only her.

"It's all right, sweetness," I said. "I done killed the little double-crossing bastard. He won't threaten you no more, I promise you that. And I don't hate you, and I don't want no divorce neither. Don't cry now, baby doll. Everything's okay."

"Oh, Barjack," she said, daubing some more at her eyes, "I do love you."

"And I love you, you most wonderful of all wonderfulnesses," I said, and then we kissed, the most passionate kiss we had ever had between us. At least it sure seemed like it at the time, and by God, my own real physical manliness was actual aroused just then of a sudden, and we didn't even bother going into the bedroom. We just got to ripping at each other's clothes, and we got after it right there on the living-room floor and on the love seat and on the dinner table and all over the damn place. I ain't never had such an experience as that in my whole entire long life of adventures and misadventures. High class, I reckon. Lord God heavenly angels above. I had me such a time as I never imagined in my most wildest dreams and imaginings. We done it and done it and done it some more. I was riding high, and she was too. I could tell that about it.

I think I won the world championship that time for long riding and repetitious shooting. I really and truly do believe it. Oh, Lordy, I felt good. I felt like I was on top of the world or riding on clouds or had died and went to heaven in spite of my many terrible sins. All my misery and shame and wretchedness from my disastrous wedding night was erased and wiped out for good and ever. I was a stud horse and a champion bull. When at last we was done, I laid back on the floor stark staring naked, near exhausted and breathing deep, trying to recover from all that grand and glorious activity, and my darling Lillian, the love of my life, was laying back on the love seat in all her undraped splendor. I never seen such a gorgeous sight before. It had been near dark in that damnable hotel room, and here we was in the middle of the day with all kinds of light just a-flooding through the windows of the house.

"Barjack," she said, and her voice was kind of husky then, "you were marvelous."

Well, that puffed me up considerable, I guess you know. I managed to pick myself up from off the floor, and I went over to set beside her and hold her close to me. Oh, that felt good.

"Well," I said, "you're the most wonderful thing that ever come along in the entire history of the whole world. Cleopatra and all them others couldn't have had nothing on you. And I ain't just sweet-talking you, neither. I mean every word I say."

She snuggled up against me real close then, and I was touching on thighs and tits and all kinds of wonderful things, and then she like to have spoiled the whole fine situation by bringing us back to the awful, impending reality of things. She said, "I'd like to just hold on to you here forever, my darling, but just look at the time."

Well, I did, and it was damn near eleven o'clock. Hell, I jumped up so fast I like to dumped my sweetness off and onto the floor. I went for my clothes real quick-like, and Lillian was getting hers together too.

"We'd better hurry," she said.

"We?" I said. "Honey sweet, I got to go face them Bensons. I don't want you getting in the way of no bullets, so you stay right here, and if I live through this thing, I'll see you a little later."

"I'm going with you," she said. "I told you I can handle a rifle. Remember? I can even handle a shotgun and a six-gun, too, if I have to."

"Lillian," I said, "I ain't going to have you—"

"Hush now," she said, and I did. "We're either going on together, or we're going out together, and that's all there is to it."

Well, I can't tell you how proud that made me feel, and how pleased I was with myself for having killed old Texas after he had gone and called her bad names. Why, it didn't make no difference to me at all no more what kind of life she had once led. By God, she was my wife, and she was the most wonderful lover I had ever had, and now she was fixing to stand up beside me in the face of terrible danger. Them Bensons was coming to town just anytime now, and she was going right along with me and shoot it out with them bastards. So to speak. I never had no intention of facing up to them fair and square, either alone or with a partner, as you well know by now.

Well, we got ourselves all dressed up, and I strapped on my two six-guns. Then I tucked a third into my belt, and I picked up the fourth to do the same with it, but Lillian held out her hand for it. I give it to her and she dropped it in her handbag. I had my right hand on the doorknob, and I give it a turn, and then I realized that we had been in there all that time doing what we was a-doing, and the goddamned door had been unlocked. That give me a sure start, but it was all right, I guess, 'cause we was all done and dressed again and still alive. Anyhow, I was fixing to pull the door open, but Lillian stepped up close and give me one last kiss on the lips. Then, "Let's go," she said. The time had come.

Chapter Twenty-one

Me and Lillian mounted up double on my tired old horse to ride back to the office, and along the way, she commenced to talking about what we was fixing to ride ourselves into. She was setting in the saddle and I was riding back behind. I held the reins, though, and done the controlling of the critter. I was that much of a gentleman. So she was talking at me back over her shoulder.

"They'll probably go straight to your office," she said. "Their only reason for coming to town is to get you."

"Yeah," I said, "that's likely just what they'll do. After a day on the trail, and that right after getting let out of old Dick Custer's jail, they might want some whiskey, all right, but most likely they'll want to get me dead first."

"Well, then," she said, "we'll just have to get ready for them. We won't be in your office. We'll be hidden somewhere nearby where we can see them, but they won't see us."

I couldn't hardly believe what it was I was hearing. Why, this woman was even more wonderful than what I had thought before. When it come right down to dry-gulching, she was of the same mind as what I was. I loved her most double when I heard that. She went on with her plan.

"We'll each have rifles," she said. "I expect that four men coming to town for a shoot-out will plan on pulling out their revolvers. Am I right about that? We'll have the advantage with rifles. From our hiding places, which I think should be one on each side of the street, we'll be able to pick them off their horses with no trouble at all."

"That sounds real reasonable to me," I said, and it sure as hell did. 'Course, I'd have liked it a whole lot better if we had six men with rifles on each side of the street, but I didn't have no twelve men, not nomore, so her plan would just have to do. I figured that if I was to shoot without giving no warning, I could most likely knock two men off their horses before they could start in to reacting. Lillian had said that she could handle a rifle, and if she really could, she ought to be able to do the same thing. From what I'd learned about her so far, I couldn't think of no reason to doubt her word.

We rode real slow down the street to my office. My old horse wouldn't hardly pick up his feet. I guess I couldn't blame him none, considering what all I had put him through already that morning. But we was just going along real slow and easy-like, and just as we was riding along in front of the Hooch House, old Bonnie came out the front door with a shotgun in each hand. Well, I roared out at the top of my voice, "Run for cover," and I throwed myself off the back of that old horse and went to rolling in the dirt, expecting a shotgun blast to follow me just any second, but none come.

I was laying there in the dirt on my face, and when I seen how quiet things was, I lifted my head up real slow-like to take a look, and there was Bonnie just standing by my horse and looking up at Lillian. She was holding both of them guns down by her sides, not menacing no one at all. Then I heard her say, "Mrs. Barjack?"

"Please," said Lillian, "call me Lillian."

"Well, we ain't met," Bonnie said, "but I'm your husband's business partner. Bonnie Boodle's my name."

Lillian got down off the old horse all by herself and stood there right in front of Bonnie.

"I'm pleased to meet you," she said.

"Me and Barjack used to be more than just business associates," Bonnie went on, "but that's all over now. He's a worthless son of a bitch, and I don't know what you want with him, but you've got him."

"Yes," said Lillian. "I do."

"Well, anyway," Bonnie said, "it's getting along toward high noon, and them Bensons will be here just anytime now, coming in to kill him. I tried to kill him myself once or twice, but now that it's near time and everyone else has run out on him, I don't want to see it happen. Not that way. So I come to help."

Well, by God, old Bonnie had came through in the pinch after all. I couldn't hardly believe what I was hearing. I figured she'd try again to kill me, and if she done it right this time, she'd tie into Lillian with her claws. But she never. I stood up and brushed myself off and walked on over to stand there beside Lillian. I was still a bit cautious about Bonnie with them guns, but she wasn't lifting up their business ends, and basic I believed what she had just said. To try to cover up my nervousness, I fired me up a cigar, but she didn't even look at me at all, though. She was still just looking right at Lillian.

"Barjack," she said, not moving her gaze at all toward me, "I guess I can't really blame you none. She is lovely."

"Uh, yeah," I said.

"Thank you," Lillian said. "I hope we can become friends."

"Yeah," Bonnie said. "Well, what are we going to do here? Time's getting short."

By God, she was right about that. "We was heading down to the office to fetch us some rifles and scope out some good hidey-holes," I said.

"All right," said Bonnie. "Let's go, then."

The three of us together walked the rest of the way on down to the office, and I reckon my old horse was grateful for at least that much relief. When we got there, I slapped his reins around the hitching rail out front. Then we went on inside to pick out our weapons. I had always had a preference for a Henry, but Lillian selected a Winchester for herself. Bonnie said she'd stick to them scatterguns. I checked both rifles over real good for their workings and made sure they was both loaded up full. Bonnie said that the shotguns was both in good order, and I just took her word for that.

We laid both of them rifles and one shotgun there on my desk. Bonnie wouldn't turn loose of the other one, and then we went back outside to study up on the possible hiding spots. Our Watering Hole building was just almost direct across the street from my office, and we decided that Bonnie would go in there. No one would pay it no mind. It looked just like what it was: an empty and boarded-up old building.

There was a real narrow space between my office and the building right next to it. It didn't have much more room that what was needed for me to squeeze my way through it sideways, and it was dark in there. It was all shadow. Lillian said that it was too tight a fit for me, so she said that she would snug herself in there. She tried it out, too, to make sure that she'd be able to maneuver around enough with a rifle, and she seen that she could, so that was settled. That left just only me to figure out what to do with. Well, Lillian stepped out into the middle of the street and looked first one way and then the other.

"Barjack," she said, "I think that you should go way down the street there to just about in front of the farm implements store. The Bensons will ride in from the opposite direction, and you'll be able to see them coming right away. Wait until they ride up even with Harvey's, and then step right out into the middle of the road. Call out to them if you have to in order to get their attention. When they see you standing there ready for them, they'll come riding your way."

"You want me to just stand right out smack in the middle of the street and be a target for them bastards?" I said.

"You won't be within range of their revolvers until they

get all the way down here to your office," she said. "Just before they get here, run for cover. Then Bonnie and I will open up on them."

"Just like that," I said.

"Just like that," she said. "It will work. Don't worry."

I didn't like it much, but, hell, I couldn't think of nothing else, so I agreed on it with her. Bonnie was real enthusiastic about it, though, and I wondered if maybe she wasn't secretly hoping that I'd get myself killed by that method, in spite of her acting like she didn't feel that way no more. Well, I'd been feeling pretty good, but just then it come to me that I still might likely be dead before this thing was over with, and I sure wanted me a glass of whiskey before the end come happening to me. I just blew out a couple of puffs of smoke and kept myself quiet.

"Let's get our rifles and get ready," Lillian said, so we all three walked on back inside the office, but instead of just picking up my old Henry, I walked on around to the back side of the desk. "What are you doing now, Barjack?" Lillian asked me.

"Well, there's fixing to be some killing here," I said. "I always like to have myself a drink just before that happens."

I pulled open my desk drawer to get the bottle and the glasses out, and then I seen them dynamite sticks again. In all my drunkenness and other distractions, I had forgot all about them. I wondered if there wasn't some way I could make use of them damn things to make matters just a little bit easier on us, but I had really picked them up thinking that I'd be using them out on the ranch. I had my fingers wrapped around one of them, but then I put it back down. Nah, I told myself, dynamite wasn't no good to use on human beings—not in town, anyhow. Out on the road, maybe. Anyhow, my mind was too much on the whiskey right then, so I just pulled it and the glasses on out and poured us each a drink. I knowed that old Bonnie could handle that stuff all right, but I was a little surprised at the easy way Lillian swallowed hers down. And I had been thinking of her as a champagne lady. Well, hell, I was sure learning a lot that day. She looked over at the clock, which was setting on eleven-forty-eight, banged her empty glass down on the desktop, and said, "Let's go."

Biting down on my cigar, I picked up my Henry. Lillian took up her Winchester, and Bonnie grabbed the extra shotgun, so that she had one in each hand again. Lillian was the first one out the door, with Bonnie right on her tail, so whenever Lillian stopped dead in her tracks, Bonnie like to have ran over her.

"Get back in," Lillian said, and them two women was back inside the office in no time. Lillian pulled the door shut quick behind her. "They're here already," she said. "It's too late. They saw me too. There's no way we can get out now to our hiding places."

"What are we going to do, then?" Bonnie said.

"We'll just have to fight it out from here," said Lillian. "Knock the glass out of these front windows."

"Wait up," I said. I'd had me a sudden brilliant thought, the way I most always do just before someone's fixing to do me something desperate. Actual, I'd had the thought before, but I had rejected it. Now there didn't seem to be no other choice. "Let's all get out the back door."

The two women went running down the hallway, and I stopped back by my desk to open the drawer again, and I reached in for the blasting sticks. I grabbed three of them and headed for the back. Lillian and Bonnie was already out in the alley ahead of me. Lillian was carrying her Winchester, and Bonnie was still lugging along both them scatterguns. I had not bothered picking up my Henry. I figured them sticks would be all I'd need. The three of us was standing just outside the back door, and I turned immediate to my left. The next door building there was a two-story one, and that was just what I wanted. I knowed that it had a back stairway, too.

Well, I hustled me on up there to the landing, and I went and reached for the overhang of the roof up there to grab onto and heave myself up with, but I was too damn short to reach it. I couldn't make it. I looked down at the women below me in the alley. "How far down the street was they?" I asked.

"They hadn't yet reached the Hooch House," Lillian said, "and I think they're walking their horses easy. They were when I saw them."

"What are you trying to do, Barjack?" Bonnie asked me.

"I want to get up on this here roof," I said, "but I can't reach the son of a bitch."

"Well, just a minute," she said, and she come hustling up them stairs, and when she got to the landing with me, she got down on her hands and knees. Well, I'd sure enough seen old Bonnie in that posture a good many times before, but never all dressed and never for such a reason as it was then. "Go on," she said, "hurry up," and I stepped up onto her back, and then I clumb real easy on up onto the roof. I could hear the stomping sound of Bonnie going back down, and I heard Lillian say to her, "Come on." Well, they went one to each side of that building and moved down to the front corners. 'Course, I didn't know that at the time. I was too busy easing my way to the front of that roof, and I sure couldn't see down off the sides of the building.

Well, the damn building had one of them false fronts on it, you know, so that whenever I reached the front of the roof, it was like I had me a wall to hide behind. I peeked real cautious up over the wall and looked down into the street. Lillian was right. Them four goddamned Bensons was moving slow and cautious down the street and coming toward us. They had reached just about the halfway mark between Harvey's Hooch House and my marshaling office, and each one of them had a shooter in his hand, and they was looking around at every corner and every window and every shadow, hunting for me lurking somewhere, I knowed. I puffed on my cigar and waited, and I recollect wondering if they would take notice of my cigar smoke curling up from behind the false front of that building there.

They moved on up to where they was just about to go past old Peester's law office, and I figured I could make a heave that distance. I touched my cigar's flame to a short fuse and waited a few seconds. If you ain't never done it, I can tell you that holding on to one of them red sticks with that fuse a-fizzing and sparking is a real unsettling experience. When I couldn't stand it no more, I throwed that son of a bitch as far as I could, and damned if I didn't overthrow them Bensons, and that death stick landed just right there at old Peester's front door. And then, KERBLOOIE, the damned thing went off, and it was like all hell and damnation had landed right there in the street. It was like twenty-seven bolts of lightning and twenty-seven claps of thunder had all struck at once right there in that same exact spot. I seen blasting before, but never like that. Never that close and right down in the middle of town. And I felt it too, way over there where I was at.

Well, I peeked up over the edge of the wall and squinted down at that place, but I couldn't see much except for smoke and dust and flying bits and pieces of wood and stuff, which I figured was old Peester's front door and wall and all that, and I did see four horses and four Bensons go scattering. I seen the horses kind of raise up their ass ends like they'd been kicked in their rears by some invisible giant's foot, and I seen all four Bensons go flying high, but then the dirty cloud sort of obscured my seeing much of anything else for a minute or two. Soon it cleared off some, though. Two horses was laying dead. The other two was running loose and scared most nearly to death. Sure enough, old Peester's whole damn front wall was gone.

Then I seen Little Red on his hands and knees, and he was scampering right down the middle of the street like a kid what hadn't learned to walk yet, not even running for cover. I reckon the blast had addled his brain somewhat. I seen another Benson just laying there like he was done for. Then I seen one come crawling off the sidewalk on the other side of the street. He straightened himself up and kind of shook his head a bit. Then he seen Little Red, and he run after him calling his name. Little Red just kept crawling. Neither one of them seemed to have no six-gun in hand after the big blast.

"Little Red, wait up," that other one was calling, and he

was about to catch up with Little Red when I tossed another stick over the side. I hadn't really tried to do it, but the damn thing landed right on Little Red's back. The other fellow stopped still for a couple of seconds, then he grabbed up that stick, but he looked around trying to decide what to do with it, I guess, only he took just a tad too long in deciding. I ducked back behind the wall again, and there was another hellacious roar, and I never seen no more of either one of them two boys.

Well, I looked and I waited, 'cause there was only three of them four accounted for, but after a while I figured that the fourth one must actual have been the first to go. That first blast, I reckoned, had blowed him clean away and likely we'd never even see the pieces. I decided to go on back down. I did have one more stick of that devil powder on me, but I just tucked it into the inside pocket of my coat. I went back to the back side of the building where I had started from, eased myself over the edge, and dropped down to the landing. I turned around to start down the stairs, and there the son of a bitch was, right down at the first step, looking up at me and pointing his ugly old Navy Colt. I reckoned it was primed and ready to go, though. Well, I just stopped still.

"You sorry-ass bastard," he said. "You done blowed my brothers all into kingdom come."

"Or some place," I said.

"I'm going to kill you, Barjack," he said, "but I ain't going to do it all at once. Not after all the damn things you done to my family. I'm going to shoot you first in the leg, and that one'll be for Vance."

"Before you do all that," I said, "just which one are you?"

"What?" he said, wrinkling his face up.

"Which one of the Bensons are you?" I asked again. "I kind of like to know who's fixing to kill me."

"Oh, well, I'm Grem," he said.

"Grem?" I said. "Was two of them out there called Loren and Orren?"

187

"That's right," said Grem, "and I'm going to shoot you once for each one of them, too."

"My old deputy, Texas Jack Dooly, told me your name was Elmo," I said.

"Well, he's a lying son of a bitch," Grem said.

"I don't know where he got his information from," I said, "but he most usual had pretty good sources. He said it was Little Red, Loren, Orren, and Elmo would be coming to town."

"I ain't Elmo," Grem said. "I don't even like that stupid name."

"Well, if you ain't Elmo," I said, "where is he?"

"There ain't no goddamned Elmo," Grem said. "To hell with your depitty. I think I'll just kill him too when I'm done with you."

"You're too late," I said. "I done killed the sorry bastard."

Old Grem kind of wrinkled up his face. "You killed your own depitty?" he said.

"That's right," I said. "Deader than hell."

"How come you to do a thing like that?" old Grem asked me. He seemed truly puzzled by my confession.

"He said some bad things about my wife," I told him. It was half the truth.

"Well, if he said bad things about your wife, and you killed him for it, how come you believed him about Elmo?" Grem wanted to know.

"I never said them bad things wasn't the truth," I told him. "Anyhow, he was trying to make me get out of town before you boys showed up, and I didn't want to do that. I was too anxious to see you after all these years that has gone by. How did you boys get along up there in the state pen, anyhow? Is it true what they say about lonely men in there?"

Well, now, you might think that I was pretty bold talking to old Grem the way I was, but the truth is I was just saying anything I could think of to keep him from shooting me any too soon. I was hoping that someone would come along before he got around to it. But that last remark I had made had went just a little too far. It really set him off, and I figured later, when I'd had time to think about it, that someone up there in the pen must have done that to him for it to make him that mad.

"You goddamn rat's ass," he shouted at me, and he raised up that old Navy shooter and aimed it right at my guts, and I figured that was the end of old Barjack right then and there. I thought about taking back what I had just said to him and trying to drag the conversation on a little while longer, but I never had the chance. He pulled the trigger, and there wasn't nothing but a click. He looked at that shooter like it had betrayed him, which I guess it had, but I figured that the explosion must have blowed the cap off of that ancient damned Colt of his. He thumbed back the hammer again and looked at the thing, and I guess he seen a cap on the next tit. He grinned and took aim again, and just then old Bonnie, God bless her fat ass and her lovely soul, come around the corner and pointed one of them scatterguns of hers and, without no hesitation at all, pulled the trigger.

Great glory, old Grem flew halfway up the stairs. I looked down at what was left of him, and it was a mess. Bonnie's shot had caught him high between the shoulder blades and in the neck, and his head was just barely hanging on. Old Bonnie, who had just earlier that same day tried four times to blow me away with a shotgun blast, had just done that very thing to Grem, the last of the Bensons, and in so doing, she had, by God, saved my ass. I heaved me a real big sigh, and then I started slow down the stairs. I had a time stepping over what was left of old Grem and not slipping on his blood, but I made it. Bonnie was just standing there a-trembling with her mouth hanging open. About that time Lillian come running from around the other corner. When I got to the ground, she come up to me and flung her arms around my neck and hugged me tight.

"Barjack," she said, "it's over."

"Yeah," I said, "and thanks to old Bonnie there, I'm still standing up."

About then Bonnie commenced to really trembling and

sobbing. "I ain't never killed a man before," she said, and me and Lillian both went over to her and held on to her, trying to calm her down. I took the shotgun out of her hands, and I was wondering, when she had been shooting at me with those damn scatterguns, if she had hit me, would she have been crying like this?

"It's all right, Bonnie," Lillian said. "You just did what you had to do. It's over now, and we won."

Chapter Twenty-two

Well, you might think the story is all over and done with. I did too, and I was sure feeling relieved, I can tell you. Old Bonnie was so upset, having just blowed old Grem Benson all to hell and blazes, that Lillian said she was going to walk her back to the Hooch House. I thought that, being town marshal and all, I had ought to go back out into the street and kind of check things out. I didn't really expect to see much left of Little Red and whichever one of the others it was that had picked up that damn stick off his back. But there was that one laying out there in the street, and I knowed that old Peester wouldn't be too pleased at my leaving dead folks around town like that. Well, by God, I got out there, and I didn't see him nowhere.

I wondered if maybe I had been mistook in what I thought I seen before. That had been a hell of a damn big and surprising explosion. I might have just thought that I seen one of them laying there dead. And then my attention had been took away by the sight of Little Red scampering down the street. Hell, I told myself, likely the first blast blowed that one all to hell, just like the second blast done to them other two. Still, I felt a little nervous, and I looked up and down the street for any sign of danger. I couldn't see no Benson, dead or otherwise. Checking my favorite Merwin and Hulbert Company revolver to make sure it was sliding easy in its holster, I took a stroll on down to old Peester's office, or at least what had been his office, and I looked in there where his front wall had used to be.

Well, I can tell you, the whole office was a wreck, and it really done my heart and soul good to see it. I couldn't think of nothing more suitable to happen to a shyster lawyer. I stepped inside kind of cautious-like,'cause I didn't want no loose boards to fall down on me. It was dusty in there, and it made me sneeze. I wiped my nose on my sleeve and stepped in a little deeper. Peeking on into the main office in the back, I seen Peester's feet sticking up on top of his desk. The rest of him was back behind it.

"Peester?" I said, and I heard a moan. I went on back there to look, and there he was. He had been blowed over on his back, and he was pretty much covered up with trash, but he seemed to be all in one piece. I throwed the trash off him, and I could see that he was black all over from the powder blast, and his suit was kind of raggedy.

"You all right?" I asked him.

"What the hell happened out there?" he said.

"The Bensons," I said. "That's what."

"Is it over?" he asked me.

"Yeah," I said. "It's over."

"Help me up," he said, "but be careful. I think my arm is broken."

Well, I got old Peester out of there and over to Doc Twitty, who was mainly the horse doctor and town barber, but also the only sorry excuse we had for a folks doctor, and then I went back outside. I headed back toward my office, still puzzling over that last Benson body, or at least what I thought should have been a body. I just couldn't figure it out. As I got closer to my office, I seen that my old horse was just laying there dead. I looked him over pretty good and couldn't see where he'd been hurt any. He was far enough away from the shocks of both blasts to be safe, I thought. I reckoned then that I had just actual rode him to death that day. It had just took him a while to go on ahead and drop. I went on inside the office, and then I sure as hell got a shock. I reckon I've got a damned strong heart. Otherwise the start of what happened would have killed me.

An arm went around my throat from behind, and a hand come up with a knife ready to plunge it down into my chest. I grabbed the wrist of the knife hand, but the other arm was choking me pretty good. I knowed it was the other Benson, even though I hadn't rightly seen him yet. Well, I guess it would have been a sight to see if there had been anyone around to see it, that Benson trying to stab me and choke me to death at the same time, and me trying to hold that knife away and still clenching my good cigar in my teeth. I reckon my face was getting red, too, from the choking.

We staggered around the room some, struggling with each other, knocking into things and growling at one another, and eventual we tumbled over the chair what stood there in front of my desk. Well, we took a hard fall, me landing on top of him and knocking out all his breath, and that made him let loose of my throat. I took advantage of the new situation and hurried up to my feet. Then I quick stepped on his right wrist to disable his knife-wielding hand. He was looking up at me with hate and killing in his eyes, but he hadn't recovered none of his breath yet, so there wasn't much he could do. I quick pulled that last stick of dynamite out of my coat, and I stuck my cigar fire to its fuse. I tell you what, his eyes got big, and his mouth dropped open even more than what it had been from just trying to gulp air. I never seen such terrible fright on a human face before. It kind of tickled me, being as how them Bensons had put me in such a state for so long.

So I let that fuse burn down real short, till it most scared me to be holding it, and then I reached down and grabbed ahold of the waistband of his britches and lifted his ass clear up off the floor, and that made a space there between his britches and his belly, and I tucked that lit stick right down the front of his pants. Then I turned and run like hell out the front door. I was just off the sidewalk when the damn thing blowed, and by God, it throwed me all the way clean across the street and rolled me up on the board sidewalk over there, and pieces of the jailhouse rained down on the street for a while. Well, for damn sure there wasn't no Bensons left after that.

There ain't much left to tell now for sure. Old Peester and the town council never did ask me too many questions about all them explosions, and I was glad of that. Whenever they did ask me something about the damn mess on our main and only street, I just only said that it was the goddamned Bensons, and of course, everyone had expected all along that all hell would break loose whenever them bastards got to town. I guess they just figured that it sure enough had and decided to let it go at that. Neither Bonnie nor Lillian never told them no different neither, and there wasn't no one else alive who seen what happened. Everyone had been hiding in as deep a hole as he could find until the fight was all over, so there weren't really no witnesses, other than just the three of us. The town like to went broke building itself a new jailhouse and paying that damn Peester off for the damages done on his office. There was some little other damage, too. Some windows blowed out and such. Peester give me hard looks every time he seen me after that, but he never direct accused me of nothing. I do believe, though, that he really did wish I had left town the way he had told me I ought to do. Either that or got myself killed.

But as far as my marshaling job is concerned, why, I come out in jim-dandy form. Since everyone in town had been hiding away and no one had seen nothing, then, like I said, all they knowed about the big fight was that the bad-ass Bensons had come to town and like to blowed the whole town up trying to kill me, and that I had got them all instead, and that I had did it all by my own lonesome self. Well, if I had been thought to be a hero when I arrested them all that other time, well, I can tell you, I was really

a hero after this last fight. Hell, I was damn near a god.
That's with a little g, you know, like old Mars and them
kind of guys in the books about them old-time Greeks. I
even begun to feel a little Greekish.

And old Bonnie never did give me no more trouble. We
stayed business partners, but only, I never hardly had to
really deal direct with her after that, 'cause her and Lillian
become the goddamndest best of friends, and together they
looked after Harvey's as well as the new hotel, which we
damn well did establish, and which we called it the Prairie
Palace. It cost me a fortune, too. Lillian took Bonnie with
her on a buying trip back east to furnish the place, and they
had so much fun that time that they took to making regular
trips east to shop for dresses and hats and such stuff as
women likes to spend their money on.

I actual begun to believe that poor old Texas and that
son of a bitch Dick Custer had figured things right whenever they said that Lillian had really married me for my
property and wealth. She had been run out of towns so
many times that she was hunting herself a sucker to settle
down with, one who could support her in a real fine way.
High fashion and social standing and such was important
to her. It surprises me a little to admit it, but it really didn't
bother me none to come to that discovery.

I probably never would have got myself to work on that
damned old ranch, but only eventual, sure enough, Lillian
come up pregnant, and I'll be damned straight down to the
very bottom of the deepest pit in hell if she didn't come
out with twins, a boy and a girl, and I had me two little fat
snotnoses running around the house. I couldn't hardly stand
it, so I went to work fixing up the ranch, and I went into
the cattle business in a big and serious way. It kept me
away from home a lot, where if I stayed, I usual just wound
up washing the dishes anyhow, and I actual started into
making some money off of cows. But I hired me some
cowboys to do the cow work, just like I had always said I
would. Everything was going my way, sure enough, except
only that married life wasn't what I had figured on it being.
I learned to live with it, though.

*   *   *

Then one day, it was 'long about quitting time, old Harrison Dingle come a-running into the new marshaling office, and I happened to be setting in there at my desk. He was waving a book in his hand, and he was real excited.

"Marshal Barjack," he was shouting. "Marshal Barjack."

"Slow down there, Dingle," said I. "What the hell's getting up your ass?"

He stopped still right in front of my desk, a-panting for his breath. "Here," he said. "Here," and he was kind of jabbing that book at me. Well, it wasn't just his own old notebook he had there. It was a real honest-to-God book, a published book from New York City.

"What's that you got there?" I asked him.

Finally he had sort of caught his breath, and he leaned forward and real gentle-like laid that book on the desk right under my nose. THE BRAVE MARSHAL: OR, BARJACK AND THE NOTORIOUS BENSON GANG was printed in real big letters right across its front cover, and then there was a real exciting picture of a feller in a black suit with a handlebar mustache and a black hat on his head and a gun a-blazing in each hand, and I reckoned that it was supposed to be me. Well, it wasn't too far off. It was a pretty dashing figure, all right. In the background, coming right at him, was four of the meanest, ugliest sons of bitches anyone ever drawed. They was all on horseback, and they was shooting guns and throwing sticks of dynamite every which way, and there was explosions going off all over the place. By God, it was a real fine drawing. Down at the bottom of the page the letters spelled out, "Written by Harrison Dingle."

I looked up at him finally when I seen that part of it. "So that's what you was up to all that time," I said. "You sure had me wondering."

"Yes, sir," he said, and he was grinning all the way across his silly face. "I hope you like it all right."

"Well," I said, "I ain't read it, of course, but it sure does look good."

"I brought that copy for you," he said.

I held the book up off the desk and studied on it real fond.

"This here's mine," I said, "to keep?"

"Yes, sir," he said.

"Well, now," I said, "that's mighty fine. I'm obliged to you, Dingle. I reckon my wife will get a kick out of this too. Yes, sir. That's a fine-looking book. A good likeness there, too, don't you think?"

"Oh yes," Dingle said. "I described you the best I could to the artist. He did a wonderful job."

"He sure as hell did," I said, and then, "Dingle," I said, "this here book come out of New York? Right?"

"Yes, sir," he said. "That's right. New York City. And it's being distributed all over the country."

"All over the whole damn country," I said, kind of musing-like. "And right there in New York City, too?"

"Yes," he said.

"And Manhattan?"

"Of course," he said, and he was grinning and nodding his head so that it looked like a cork on a fishing line.

"Well, I'll be damned," I said, and I wondered if any of my family back there which I had total lost touch with years ago would maybe pick up a copy and recognize me from it. They'd for sure take notice of the name, but I never used my first name, 'cause it was several syllables long and hard for folks to say out loud. They wouldn't recognize me from that drawing on the cover neither, since the last time they seen me I was just a raggedy-assed kid. But they might figure out from the family name that I was their long-lost kid and brother and all. Then I thought about that damn Five Points kid too, and I figured that if he was ever to get a look at that book and do the same kind of figuring and then knowed who I was, he'd feel damn lucky to still be alive, having once tangled with me. My head swelled some, and I stood up and walked around the desk. I throwed my arm around old Dingle's shoulder and started walking him toward the door. "Harrison, old partner," I said, "why don't you come on home with me and have supper with me and the wife?"

He did, and we become good buddies. He even said that his publisher wanted him to write some more books about me. And Lillian did like it too, especial when Dingle told us that there would be some money in it for me too, not just only him for the writing of it. I felt pretty good about all that for a little while, but then one otherwise fine day a young punk with two guns tied to his legs and hanging way down low come riding into town. He said he was looking for me, and I seen right away that what he was really looking for was he was looking for a reputation as a fast gunnie, and most likely he had read that damn book. Well, I wasn't about to give him a chance to achieve his desire over my dead body, so whenever he stood out in the street in front of the Hooch House and hollered for me to come out and shoot it out with him, I went out the back door, walked around the building, and snuck up on him from his backside. I cracked his skull with the barrel of my Merwin and Hulbert Company, self-extracting, forty-five-caliber revolver, and while he was still out cold, I stomped on his both hands with my boot heels, breaking every damn bone they had in them. He'd never give me nor no one else no more gunfighting trouble.

But the real hell of it was that I seen right then and there that I had bought myself some big trouble when I had wiped out them Bensons, and whenever old Dingle went and wrote that goddamned book, which I admit that I liked right well at first, and then, worse, went and got it published and sent out all over the country for everyone to see, well, that just made matters worse by about one hundred and fifty-seven times. I knowed that gunfighting kid was only the first one. He damn sure wouldn't be the last.

Oh, yeah, in case you've been wondering about poor old Tootie Harman, she come out all right. She went to work for Bonnie in the Hooch House, and she's doing right well.

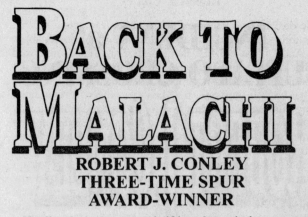

INCIDENT at BUFFALO CROSSING

ROBERT J. CONLEY

The Sacred Hill. It rose above the land, drawing men to it like a beacon. But the men who came each had their own dreams. There is Zeno Bond, the settler who dreams of land and empire. There is Mat McDonald, captain of the steamship *John Hart*, heading the looming war between the Spanish and the Americans. And there is Walker, the Cherokee warrior called by a vision he cannot deny—a vision of life, death...and destiny.

___4396-3 $4.50 US/$5.50 CAN

THE ACTOR

ROBERT J. CONLEY

Bluford Steele had always been an outsider until he found his calling as an actor. Instead of being just another half-breed Cherokee with a white man's education, he can be whomever he chooses. But when the traveling acting troupe he is with arrives in the wild, lawless town of West Riddle, the man who rules the town with an iron fist forces them to perform. Then he steals all the proceeds. Steele is determined to get the money back, even if it means playing the most dangerous role of his life—a cold-blooded gunslinger ready to face down any man who gets in his way.

___4498-6 $4.50 US/$5.50 CAN

Dorchester Publishing Co., Inc.
P.O. Box 6640
Wayne, PA 19087-8640

Please add $1.75 for shipping and handling for the first book and $.50 for each book thereafter. NY, NYC, and PA residents, please add appropriate sales tax. No cash, stamps, or C.O.D.s. All orders shipped within 6 weeks via postal service book rate. Canadian orders require $2.00 extra postage and must be paid in U.S. dollars through a U.S. banking facility.

Name_____

Address_____

City_____State_____Zip_____

I have enclosed $_____ in payment for the checked book(s).

Payment <u>must</u> accompany all orders. ☐ Please send a free catalog.

CHECK OUT OUR WEBSITE! www.dorchesterpub.com

ELIZABETH, BY NAME
WILL COOK

Bestselling Author Of *Sabrina Kane*

IN THE EARLY DAYS OF THE TEXAS TERRITORY, ONLY THOSE WITH COURAGE AND STRENGTH CAN SURVIVE....

There is a cattle crossing at Mustang Creek. It is miles from anywhere, and no one has ever lived there—until Elizabeth Rettig comes. Since she knows the Texans will be driving their great herds of longhorns by on the way to Dodge, she sets up a trading post.

The territory is plagued by deadly tornadoes, burning summers, and freezing winters. Indians and trail hands and vicious, lawless men ride past on their way to fame or infamy. And because Elizabeth is young and spirited, suitors come too. But only the man with the strength to tame the wild land—and the patience to outlast Elizabeth's stubbornness—will win her heart.

__3868-4 $4.99 US/$6.99 CAN

MOVING ON
JANE CANDIA COLEMAN

Jane Candia Coleman is a magical storyteller who spins brilliant tales of human survival, hope, and courage on the American frontier, and nowhere is her marvelous talent more in evidence than in this acclaimed collection of her finest work. From a haunting story of the night Billy the Kid died, to a dramatic account of a breathtaking horse race, including two stories that won the prestigious Spur Award, here is a collection that reveals the passion and fortitude of its characters, and also the power of a wonderful writer.

___4545-1 $4.99 US/$5.99 CAN

Dorchester Publishing Co., Inc.
P.O. Box 6640
Wayne, PA 19087-8640

Please add $1.75 for shipping and handling for the first book and $.50 for each book thereafter. NY, NYC, and PA residents, please add appropriate sales tax. No cash, stamps, or C.O.D.s. All orders shipped within 6 weeks via postal service book rate. Canadian orders require $2.00 extra postage and must be paid in U.S. dollars through a U.S. banking facility.

Name_____
Address_____
City_____State_____Zip_____
I have enclosed $_____ in payment for the checked book(s).
Payment <u>must</u> accompany all orders. ❑ Please send a free catalog.
       CHECK OUT OUR WEBSITE! www.dorchesterpub.com

DAVY CROCKETT

BLOOD HUNT

David Thompson

With only his oldest friend and his trusty long rifle for company, Davy Crockett explores the wild frontier looking for adventure, and has the strength and cunning to face any enemy. But even he may have met his match when he gets caught between two warring tribes on one side and a dangerous band of white men on the other—all of them willing to die—and kill—for a group of stolen women. It is up to Crockett to save the women, his friend and his own hide if he wants to live to explore another day.

_4229-0 $3.99 US/$4.99 CAN

A BALLAD FOR SALLIE

JUDY ALTER

Longhair Jim Courtright has been both a marshal and a desperado—and in Hell's Half Acre, the roughest part of Fort Worth, he is a living legend. His skill with a gun has made him a hero in some people's eyes . . . and a killer in others'. As soon as young widow Sallie McNutt steps off the stage from Tennessee, her refined manners and proper attire set her apart from the other women of the Half Acre. And it isn't long before something else sets her apart—someone wants her dead.

___4365-3 $4.50 US/$5.50 CAN

CHEYENNE

River of Death/
Desert Manhunt
Judd Cole

River of Death. Touch the Sky has gladly risked death many times over for his people, but when their worst enemies unite to deprive the Cheyennes of their life-giving river, he has to face the worst death of all: death by drowning. As the mighty shaman knows only too well, the soul of a Cheyenne who drowns can never cross to the Land of Ghosts, but must remain forever trapped, alone in the river of death . . .

And in the same action-packed volume . . .

Desert Manhunt. In an attempt to murder Touch the Sky, Big Tree infiltrated his camp and flung one of his razor-sharp blades at him before fleeing for his life. But he does not count on Touch the Sky's beloved wife throwing herself in front of the blade. Touch the Sky vows to make Big Tree's world a hurting place—a vow that only one of them can survive!

___4676-8 $4.99 US/$5.99 CAN

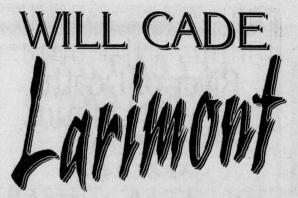

WILL CADE
Larimont

John Kendall doesn't want to go back home to Larimont, Montana. He has to—to investigate the death of his father. At first everyone believed that Bill Kendall died in a tragic fire… until an autopsy reveals a bullet hole in Bill's head. But why is the local marshal keeping it a secret? John isn't quite sure, so he sets out to find the truth for himself. But the more he looks into his father's death, the more secrets he uncovers—and the more resistance he meets. It seems there are a whole lot of folks who don't want John nosing around, folks with a whole lot to lose if the truth comes out. But John won't stop until he digs up the last secret. Even if it is one better left buried.

___4618-0 $4.50 US/$5.50 CAN